19 RAILWAY STREET

19 RAILWAY STREET

MICHAEL SCOTT
and
MORGAN LLYWELYN

POOLBEG

Published 1996 by
Poolbeg Press Ltd,
123 Baldoyle Industrial Estate,
Dublin 13, Ireland

A catalogue record for this book is available from the British Library.

ISBN 1 85371 642 1

Cover illustration by Alex Callaway
Cover design by Poolbeg Group Services Ltd
Set by Poolbeg Group Services Ltd in Goudy 11.5/14.5
Printed and bound in Great Britain by
Cox & Wyman Ltd, Reading, Berks.

About the Authors

Michael Scott is an internationally renowned writer. He has written over forty books. *Vampyre*, his first novel with Poolbeg was published in 1995.

Morgan Llywelyn was born in New York City. A prolific writer of adult books, her books for children include *Brian Boru* and *Strongbow*. *Cold Places*, her first novel with Poolbeg was published in 1995.

CHAPTER ONE

19 Railway Street
1907

Pressing his forehead to the peeling wooden door, Mickser Lawless squeezed his eyes shut and prayed to a God he wasn't sure he believed in anymore.

"Please God, don't let me Daddy die."

He concentrated on the words, repeating them slowly, using every effort of his will to force the words up to God. This wasn't real praying, he knew. Real prayers were those his mother said every night when she asked God to find a cure for Daddy, and a job, and a little money. Real prayers were those his Daddy said before each meagre meal, whether it was bread and dripping when they had no money or bacon and cabbage when they had. Real prayers were those the priest said at Mass every Sunday . . . and they must work for him, because Mickser had never seen a

1

poor or dirty priest and he was sure a priest never went hungry.

"Is Dada going to go to heaven?"

Mickser blinked his eyes clear and turned away from the door with a smile on his thin face. He sat on the top stair between his younger brother and sister and put an arm around each of them. Emma, the baby, was only four, but Thomas was eight and knew how serious the situation was. Doctors only came to the tenement house when someone was very ill; the last time a doctor had been in 19 Railway Street was when old Missus White was ill just after Easter. She had lived in the front sitting-room on the ground floor – the best room in the house, she was always saying.

Two days after the doctor's visit, all the occupants of the house had attended her wake. A family of eight now occupied her room.

"Is Dada going to go to heaven?" Thomas repeated the question, blinking hard to stop the tears gathering on his thick eyelashes.

Mickser breathed in deeply, and, for an instant, the odours of the old house – rot and mould, cabbage and urine – were wiped away and all he could smell was the faintly bittersweet odour of sickness that lingered around his father's bed. "No," he said firmly, his voice louder than he intended as he desperately tried to convince himself. But he knew it was a lie.

Mickser stood alongside his mother in the doorway and listened to the doctor's footsteps clatter down the bare wooden stairs to the landing below. The sound changed briefly as they crossed the recently replaced floorboards outside Mr Mulvany's door, then the footsteps descended the next staircase and went out into the hallway. There was no scrape of the hall door opening or bang of it slamming; the door leading outside was only closed in the worst of the weather. Although November had been wet, it wasn't cold enough to close the door.

"What did he say, Mam?" Mickser asked softly, drawing his mother out onto the landing. He glanced behind him to make sure that Emma and Thomas were out of earshot. They were standing before the rickety wooden table, eating their tea: bread coated with dripping, washed down with watered milk.

Nan Lawless wrapped her arms around her body, holding herself so tightly that Mickser feared she would break. He didn't know how old his mother was – thirty-one, thirty-two, something like that – but she looked twenty years older. Mickser had inherited his thick mop of jet black hair from his mother, though now hers was iron grey shot through with white. The lines and wrinkles of a much older woman were etched into the soft flesh around her eyes and mouth. Try as he might, Mickser couldn't remember the last time he had heard her laugh.

The boy rested his hand on her forearm. He could feel her bones through the worn and frayed wool of her cardigan. "What did the doctor say?" he repeated.

Nan Lawless drew in a deep breath and rubbed at her face with the heel of her hand, roughly wiping away the tears. "It's not good," she said simply.

"Ah."

As Mickser breathed the single word, his stomach clenched with fear. In that instant he understood that everything he had known and relied upon throughout his life was gone forever. He swayed, then clutched tightly at the banister rail. The sudden dizziness passed and the world righted itself . . . but the boy knew it would never be the same again.

In his fourteen years – when everything else had changed around them, when his father lost job after job and they had been forced to move to a succession of seedier houses, in good times and in bad – his mother and father had always been there.

But not for very much longer.

And what would happen if . . . no, *when* . . . his father died? What would happen then?

"How long?" he asked. But it was a foolish question, he did not really want to know. "I mean there must be something we can do . . ."

Nan blinked furiously, determined not to allow Mickser to see her crying again. "The doctor doesn't know how long," she whispered. "It could be a month, three months, six months. If he lives through this Christmas, though, it will be a miracle."

"But there must be medicines that will make him better!" Mickser cried, his tone shrill with fear and desperation. Then he saw his younger brother and sister watching him and lowered his voice. "There must be some medicines we can get, Mam."

Nan squeezed Mickser's shoulder. "Medicines are for the rich. But more than that," she added, gesturing at the mould-streaked walls, "he needs to get away from this . . . this disease pit. We need to take your father out into the country for a period of time, years even; someplace where the air is clean and fresh. But that's not going to happen," she said bitterly. "Might as well wish for the moon." Giving a final squeeze to her son's shoulder, she returned to the single room where the family lived. From the corner close to the fire

5

sounded the pained, gurgling cough that had come to punctuate every waking moment of their lives.

"I will not let my father die," Mickser Lawless whispered to himself softly, fiercely. Like a sacred vow. But in his heart he knew his father would die . . . and there was nothing he could do about it.

CHAPTER TWO

19 Princess Sophie Mecklenburg Street
1776

By the time she returned from her afternoon carriage drive Sophie was in a temper. Sweeping through the front door, she flung off her cloak without looking around. Garrett caught it before it hit the hall floor, as he always did, but he gave the faintest of frowns to show his disapproval. As he always did.

The delicate French heels of her shoes beat an angry tattoo across the black and white squares of the marble floor. "That woman," she muttered under her breath. "That woman!" Pausing in front of the big hall mirror in its gilded frame, she glanced anxiously at her throat. But her beloved cameo was still there, secure on its velvet band. For now.

Mademoiselle would take it away from Sophie if she dared.

"That woman" wanted everything she saw. Although she had been in the house for only a few months, Mademoiselle Moulin was treating 19 Mecklenburg Street and everything it contained as if they were her personal property. Even Garrett, who had been butler to the Rutledge family for twenty-five years, would not dare to presume as she did.

And she was just a hired governess!

Things would be different, Sophie thought sadly, if Mama and Papa had not died. But ever since Cousin Robert came to live in the house a year ago and became her guardian, things had gone from bad to worse.

"He treats me as if I were a child," Sophie had complained to Cook earlier that day.

The woman working at the big deal table, her arms white to the elbow with flour, cast a fond glance at the girl. Sophie was so pretty, Cook thought, with her unblemished skin and her shining, coppery hair. Today she wore her hair brushed smoothly back and held with a taffeta bow, then cascading into glossy ringlets.

"You do be a child, lass."

"I am almost sixteen, a young woman! At my age many girls in Dublin are already married."

"I was myself," Cook had conceded. "But I was an orphan with no one to protect me; for me it was marry or . . ." She did not finish. Some things were never discussed in front of gently reared young ladies like Sophie Rutledge. Instead she busied herself with her baking.

Meanwhile Sophie had dropped onto the nearest chair and kicked her shoes across the room.

Cook sighed patiently. "Now why are you after doing that? Here, put them on again. You cannot be going around in your stocking feet, you'll catch your death." She collected the shoes and carried them back to Sophie, who refused to look at them. "I hate those shoes," the girl muttered sullenly.

"Please Miss! I shall be blamed if anyone sees you like this. Do put your shoes back on and get ready for your carriage ride, you know Mr Robert insists that you take the air in the afternoons. Please."

Sophie could not remember Cook ever sounding so nervous. Servants in the Rutledge household had always been kindly treated, almost as if they were part of the family. At least they had been until the *Duchess of Moray* sank with all hands while importing a cargo of timber for newly fashionable mahogany furniture, and the owner and his lady died with their ship leaving Sophie an orphan.

Now everything was changed. Cousin Robert had swept into the house with the intention of putting his own stamp on the place. He demanded total control and wasted no time on exchanging pleasantries with the lower classes. The servants were afraid of him.

So for Cook's sake Sophie had put on her shoes. Then she had taken her carriage ride with Mademoiselle beside her constantly correcting her posture, her gestures, even the direction in which she glanced. Mademoiselle's own glances had returned all too often, however, to Sophie's cameo. Her black eyes had glittered like those of a rat in the stable, staring at the corn.

Now as Sophie climbed the stairs she touched the cameo for reassurance. It was the last gift Papa had given her. When she was cross, he used to buy her pretty presents to coax her into a good mood. But Cousin Robert disapproved of what he called "bribes". "You are far too spoiled," he told her. "Mademoiselle agrees with me." Only he pronounced it "Mamzelle", in the French style. He liked everything French.

Sophie drove her heels angrily into the stairs as she went up to her bedchamber on the second floor.

She had always loved the house; her home. Her earliest memories were of the big sunny nursery overlooking the mews, where a cheerful fire was always burning on the hearth and Nurse used to toast bread on a long iron toasting-fork, then soak bits in her tea with a guilty giggle. On the mantelpiece stood an enamel clock in the shape of a black and white dog. In front of the hearth Sophie had her own little chair, painted bright red, and a cushion embroidered with her name. Even after she was too old for a nursery and was given a proper bedchamber, the room was kept as it was because she burst into tears at any suggestion of changing it.

But one of the first things Cousin Robert had done upon moving into the house was strip the nursery and store its contents in the attic and cellar. Sophie's tears had left him unmoved. "I need more space for myself," he had said, "and this is perfect."

So Sophie's world was diminished and her dearest memories heartlessly tossed aside.

She hated him. She could not decide who she hated more, Cousin Robert or that French woman he had brought into the house. Between them they had ruined everything.

CHAPTER THREE

The cobbles were cool beneath his bare feet, slick with accumulated grease and grime, as Mickser walked down Railway Street. He kept his head bent, eyes darting over the cobbles, looking for shards of glass or nails, anything that might cut into his feet. He'd sliced over the sole of his foot the previous year and an infection had set in almost immediately. He'd been terrified he was going to lose his foot – or even his leg – to gangrene, but one of the old women in the tenement opposite had made up a poultice of bread and sugar and that had drawn the infection.

There was an inch long scar on the underside of his foot now, but Mickser had counted himself lucky. Tommy Shaw, who was only a year older than himself, had lost his foot when he'd stepped in some horse manure, and an open cut on his big toe had gone bad. After that Tommy had used a crutch and everyone had called him Hop-a-long, until he'd slipped and fallen under a dray hauling coal.

Mickser was angry, and he wasn't entirely sure why.

He was angry with his father, though he knew that it wasn't his father's fault that he was ill. He was angry with the doctor who had said that Mickser's father was dying of consumption . . . only what was that other name he used, tuberculosis? He was angry because the family did not have enough money for proper medicine and nourishing food to help Da fight the disease. They did not even have enough to keep paying the rent on their one miserable room at 19 Railway Street for much longer.

The boy stopped walking and drew a deep breath, feeling the rage burn and boil within him. Clenching his fists, he stepped off the street and ducked into a foul-smelling alleyway. There, in private, he allowed the tears that had been gathering all day to flow. Huge, bitter sobs wracked his thin body. He wasn't crying for himself; he was crying because he knew what was coming. He had grown up in the tenements; he saw what happened to people when they were evicted. And as soon as they missed one payment on their rent . . .

The boy blinked back the tears and looked up

at the thin strip of sky that showed between the buildings. It was pale, eggshell blue now, but winter was creeping over the city. The nights were drawing in more quickly, the mornings were frosty. A hard freeze was being forecast by the old women of the neighbourhood. The air was already thick with smoke and cinders from the coal fires people were lighting.

Soon it would be Christmas.

Soon his father would die.

But before he died, Mickser's mother would have worked herself half to death, trying to earn a few coppers with which to buy medicine for him. She would starve herself so that Frank would have that little bit extra to eat. And it would all be for nothing.

His father would die, and they would be evicted into the street and left to starve.

Mickser had seen evictions before. He had stood and watched as the landlord's men had gone into other tenements and evicted other families who had fallen behind in the rent. First the people were thrown out, men shouting, women screaming, children howling. Then, while two burly men, usually accompanied by at least one policeman, stood guard in front of the door, the rest of the bailiffs would toss the few sticks of furniture out into the street. What wasn't smashed too often was stolen.

Mickser had never thought it would happen to them. Until Da took the consumption.

And nobody could help. In the part of Dublin where the Lawless family lived, people hardly had enough for themselves.

The boy pushed away from the wall and hurried down the street, heading for the quays. If a boat had come in there might be an opportunity to run a few odd jobs for the sailors, earn a ha'penny or a couple of farthings. And, sure if they weren't looking, maybe there would be an opportunity to grab a handful of fruit or a couple of lumps of coal.

Mickser blessed himself automatically as he hurried past the Pro-Cathedral in Marlborough Street . . . while simultaneously snatching an apple from the fruit-seller's cart outside the cathedral. It wasn't theft, he reasoned, slipping into the crowd, he was simply hungry, and he was sure that God wouldn't want him to go hungry. The boy caught a glimpse of himself in the window of a shop as he darted past; a mop of unruly hair dominating a too-thin face, eyes black and deep sunk in his head, shirt too small, trousers too big: he looked just like any other slum kid.

He wasn't sure that God paid too much attention to slum kids anyway.

Coming out onto the quays, the boy turned to

the left and followed the river down to the magnificent Custom House. The tide was low and the River Liffey stank of mud and refuse. Mickser sneered as a well-dressed couple hurried past with linen handkerchiefs pressed to their faces, leaving a trail of floral scent in their wake. Those two wouldn't survive in the tenements, he thought to himself, where the air was often thick as soup with the smell of too many people living together. Damp clothes, illness, filthy outhouses, rotten food – all overlaid with the disinfectant and carbolic or Dirt Shifter soap used to scrub the steps and window ledges. Even the poorest people had their pride.

But the tenements of Dublin smelled worse than the river.

A boat was just tying up as Mickser arrived and the quays were in chaos, with big burly stevedores shouting above the roar of the engines. The boy ducked through the crowd to get to the water's edge, dodging as a rope as thick as his waist was thrown down from the boat. Shading his eyes with a grubby hand, he attempted to read the name on the prow of the boat, but though the letters were English, the words were strange.

The boat was registered in Lisbon and Mickser found himself wondering where Lisbon was. It sounded so exotic. There had been a time when he dreamed of travelling, of stowing away aboard a boat like this and going to the places he had seen named on the side of ships: Cairo and Port Said, Hamburg or Valparaiso. He had no interest in visiting the more mundane places, London and New York. From all he had heard about them they sounded like Dublin, only bigger and noisier.

Mickser had even made real plans several months ago, painstakingly saving his farthings and ha'pennies and pennies until he had nearly five shillings. He had stolen a good jumper off a clothes-line in the garden of a post house in Rathmines, wrapped it around a loaf of hard bread, and then stood on the quays waiting for a boat to come in.

But the boats that day hadn't come from any of the exotic places he longed to see. So finally he went home. And that night his father had started coughing. In the morning there was dark blood on his pillow. Later that day the boy had handed over the money and the bread to his mother, and given up all his dreams of travel.

If he left who would look after his mother, brother and sister? Mickser was the man of the house now.

Turning away, he moved through the milling crowd, his eyes sharp and alert. There were boxes being unloaded off the boat, and the horse-drawn drays were beginning to line up to take the cargo to the warehouses. He saw a dray from one of the big fruit-merchants and began to sidle towards that, but the drayman spotted him and brandished his whip. Mickser pretended he hadn't seen him and allowed the crowd to swallow him up. When he glanced back, the red-faced man was busy with the first of the boxes of fruits that were being unloaded off the boat.

Fruit would be good for his father, Mickser decided.

The boy worked his way around through the crowd until he was almost directly behind the wagon, with the body of the horse between him and the drayman. The thickset roan turned its head in his direction and blinked huge eyes at him, nostrils flaring. "If I get something, I'll give you a bit," Mickser whispered.

The lip of the wagon was taller than his head. By ducking down and peering between the spokes of the wooden wheels, Mickser could see the drayman. He was picking up boxes from a pile and carrying them back to the dray. When he set down one heavy box, it took him fifteen steps to return for another.

Mickser couldn't read very well, he had to struggle with the words, but he knew how to count. He had been counting pennies almost from the day he was born; every slum kid had.

The dray rattled as another box of fruit was dropped into it. Mickser watched the big man walk away, and began to count.

"One . . . two . . . three . . ."

The boy grabbed the edge of the wheel and clambered up onto it, using the spokes as steps in a ladder.

"Four . . . five . . . six . . ."

He grabbed the first box, hissing in pain as a long splinter bit deeply into his index finger, and yanked the lid off. Even before he knew what the fruit was, he was grabbing handfuls of the paper-wrapped balls and stuffing them down the front of his shirt. A rich, mouthwatering odour suddenly washed over him and he felt his stomach rumble. Oranges. They were oranges!

"Eight . . . nine . . . ten . . ."

It took him a couple of valuable seconds to pull the top off the next box . . .

"Eleven . . . twelve . . . thirteen . . ."

Apples. Sweet, red, crisp apples. He grabbed two, shoving them into his bulging shirt, then another two . . .

"Fourteen . . . fifteen . . ."

"Hey! Hey you! What the bloody hell do you think you're doing?" Boots pounded across the cobbles.

Mickser paused only long enough to slip the horse its promised reward.

CHAPTER FOUR

After supper in the servant's hall, the staff of the Rutledge household enjoyed a brief leisure before the routine of putting the house to bed began. Garrett liked to smoke a pipe of Virginia tobacco beside the fireplace, while Cook sat opposite him, doing her personal sewing. The rest of the servants, consisting of Mrs Mayne the housekeeper, the maids, the skivvy, and Norman the coachman, tended to linger around the big table talking after their meal.

As usual, the new governess had eaten in the dining-room with Mr Robert.

This evening there was a sense of disturbance in the house that reached all the way to the servant's hall. Earlier Sophie had quarrelled with Mademoiselle. "You have no right to go through my things!" she had cried, fighting back tears. "Those are Mama's pearls, you took them from my dressing-table. Who said you could wear them?"

"You should be more generous," the Frenchwoman had replied with a sniff. "Selfishness is unbecoming in a lady. Besides, such jewels are not appropriate for a child your age."

Sophie had run to her room and slammed her door so hard it rattled the glass of the window on the stair landing. When she would not come down for her meal Cook had one of the maids carry a tray up to her, including a generous portion of her favourite strawberry fritters, but it was returned untouched.

Mr Robert was furious. "That child grows worse every day. I will not have her insulting Mademoiselle, who only wants to improve her taste and manners. I brought that woman all the way from France for Sophie's benefit, she should be grateful!"

Standing in the upstairs hall, he had shouted through the door to Sophie that she could not leave her room until she apologised to Mademoiselle. Then he strode down to the servant's hall to announce, "That girl is not to be pampered, you understand? I blame you for indulging her as you indulge yourselves. I am tempted to dismiss the lot of you. If any of you makes any further effort to encourage Sophie in her wilfulness, I shall."

Now as they sat by the fire Cook remarked to Garrett, "It would be better if Mr Robert had chosen to stay in King George's army. There's rebellion in the Colonies, he might have been sent to one of those heathenish places like Boston and trouble us no more."

"He did not leave willingly," the butler replied. "I happen to know he was cashiered out for conduct unbecoming an officer. Colonel Maunsel's butler overheard his master say that Robert Rutledge backed every slow horse in Britain, and had run up huge debts he could not pay. When he was thrown out of the army he came crawling back to Dublin with a pack of moneylenders on his heels. He hoped the family would get him out of his trouble, but instead he arrived just in time to learn of the Master's death. Now Mr Robert's managing the Rutledge shipping business. Lucky for him, you might say, but unlucky for the rest of us."

Cook nodded. "Especially Miss Sophie. Since he's been here that pretty child has grown quite thin and sallow, with the laughter gone out of her. It's worried I am, Garrett, for her sake."

"So am I," admitted the butler. He shot a quick glance down the room, but the housekeeper was engaged in a brisk argument with the coachman, while the maids cleared the table and sneaked the last of the pudding.

Leaning forward, Garrett asked Cook, "What will happen on Christmas Eve, do you suppose?"

"Miss Sophie's sixteenth birthday? Why, whether he likes it or not Mr Robert will have to give the poor dear child a party or all of Dublin society will be scandalised."

"There is more to it than that. Come with me for a moment." Garrett nodded his head in the direction of the passage. Puzzled, Cook rose and followed him to the servants' stairs at the back of the house. One flight up was the butler's pantry, behind the dining-room. At the door to the pantry Garrett took a key from his pocket, inserted it into the lock, then opened the door and gestured for Cook to enter.

She was greeted by a luxurious silence and the smell of silver polish. In addition to a vast collection of china dishes and imported glassware, the family silver was stored in the butler's pantry. There was a walk-in safe with baize-covered shelves for the most valuable pieces. More silver gleamed from glass-fronted cupboards or was arranged in cutlery drawers lined with blue flannel. Down one side of the room was a worktable well stocked with polish and soft cloths. The Rutledge silver was Garrett's personal responsibility, and he rarely allowed anyone else into the room.

"This is for your ears alone," he told Cook as

he closed the door behind her. "I happen to know something about the Master's will. I was asked to witness some changes he made to it only days before he took the Mistress on that fateful voyage. Word of Mr Robert's disgrace had troubled him greatly. Robert was the Master's last surviving male relative, so his name remained in the will as guardian for Miss Sophie. But the Master changed his bequests. Originally half of all his property would have gone to his cousin, including a controlling interest in Rutledge Shipping. But now on Sophie's sixteenth birthday the entire estate is going to her. Robert is to have only the salary he receives from the business."

Cook raised her eyebrows almost to the frill on her starched white cap. "Are you serious?"

"I am serious."

"And does Mr Robert know this?"

"He must. The Master's solicitor paid a call on him when he first came here and they spent a long time in the library with the doors closed. When they came out, Mr Robert's face was as black as thunder."

"Miss Sophie is quite unaware of it," said Cook. "Surely she would have mentioned something so important if she knew."

Garrett replied, "Children are not usually informed of financial arrangements, and she will be a child until Christmas Eve."

CHAPTER FIVE

The smell hit Mickser the moment he pushed his way through the door. His stomach gurgled, then growled alarmingly. His mouth was abruptly full of saliva. His mother was bent over the battered black pot in the fireplace. "Meat?" he asked, incredulously, swallowing hard. "You got some meat?" He peered over her shoulder into the pot, breathing deeply, inhaling the rich smell of stew.

"I got a heart from the butchers," Nan Lawless replied with a wan smile, "and carrots, potatoes, onions and turnips from the dealers in Moore Street. Some of them are a bit limp, but no matter. I thought a stew would do your father good," she added softly, glancing over to the bed in the corner of the room. Beneath the piled blankets and old coats, Frank Lawless was an indistinct shape. Only his rasping, liquid breathing marked his presence.

Mickser nodded quickly. He was almost afraid to ask where his mother had got the money for the meat. Moving over to the table, he unbuttoned his shirt and carefully picked out the apples and oranges, arranging them in a neat line on the scarred wood.

"Where did you get those?" Nan's voice was sharp with suspicion.

"There was a boat in on the quays," Mickser replied, being careful to look her in the eye. "I did a bit of running about," he added, letting his mother think he had done some errands for some of the crew, "and I got these."

It was almost the truth, he consoled himself. There was a boat, and he had certainly done some running. When his mother made him go to confession for Christmas he would explain to the priest. The priest would then give him Absolution and everything would be all right again. Besides, he reckoned, it wasn't a real lie. And surely God would want his father to have fresh fruit, which was a rare enough treat.

The boy lifted an orange, cupping it in both hands, and held it up to his mother's face. Late autumn sunlight was streaming through the window. Reflecting off the surface of the orange, it gave Nan Lawless's skin a brief, golden glow.

"Just smell this, Mam," invited the boy.

Mother and son inhaled the rich aroma of the

fruit together. "It smells of summer," Nan said finally.

"And foreign places," Mickser added. "Have you ever travelled, Mam?"

"Travelled? Travel where?" The woman turned back to the fire, lifting the lid on the pot, her head briefly enveloped in savoury steam.

"I mean, did you ever go anywhere, visit foreign places?" said Mickser, carefully cracking the skin off the largest orange. The acidic odour made his eyes water.

"Foreign places! I've never been outside of Dublin in my life." Nan stopped and considered. "If fact, I've lived my whole life within a couple of miles of this house. I was born in a house just like this one on Sarsfield Quay; my mother sold fruit off a stall in Henry Street, my father worked as a bottle washer in Bride Street. You never knew them, Mickser, they died before you were born. But they were good people, and I wish they were here now."

Ducking her head, Nan added a pinch of salt to the bubbling stew. "I married your father on the day I turned eighteen, and then you arrived two weeks before my nineteenth birthday. You were born in the house on Sarsfield Quay, but shortly after that we moved to York Street; I knew no one there and I hated it. A year later there was another baby, but she only lived a single day. We christened her Angela, because she was like a little angel. We moved again, this time to Copper Alley, and then less than a year after that, there were twins."

"I think I remember them," Mickser whispered. He had the vaguest memories of two fat-faced children lying side by side in a white-painted cot . . . and then, suddenly, one day they were gone. He remembered his mother screaming. The sound went on and on. Shortly after that the room began filling with people. Then there had been a sort of party, he dimly recalled, with two little white boxes on the floor in the corner of the room.

"Mary and Martha. They lived for three months. One night I put them to sleep, and the next morning, they were both dead. No reason, nothing wrong with them . . . they were simply gone." Nan was quiet for a long time while Mickser concentrated on the orange, convincing himself that his eyes were watering from the smell of the juice.

"I think it might have had something to do with all the moving around," his mother remarked at last. "We were always moving in those days."

"Why?" Mickser wondered. He broke open a segment of orange and brought it to his mother, popping it into her open mouth before she could protest.

Nan glanced sidelong at her husband and sighed. "Your Daddy doesn't drink now. But there was a time, when he worked on the docks, when he had a terrible problem with the drink. You see, dockers were paid in the pubs on a Friday morning. The barmen encouraged it, of course, and the stevedores who handed out the wages were often given free drink if they paid their men in a particular pub. Once the men had their money very little of it actually left the premises. Often your father would come in on a Friday evening having spent most of his money on drink."

Mickser bit into his piece of orange. The juice flooded his mouth, but it tasted strangely sour. He wondered why his mother, who had never spoken about this before, was telling him now. Did it have something to do with his father's illness? He wasn't sure.

Nan pulled up a chair and sat at the table. Picking up a piece of orange skin, she rubbed it against the palm of her hand, soothing the work-callused flesh with orange oil. "We were always behind on the rent," she continued, "but we managed to stay one step ahead of the bailiff. Then when the twins died, your father changed. I know he blamed himself for a long time. He thought if he had given me more money, I would have been able to get them better food. But I'm sure he was wrong. It wasn't his fault."

Mickser nodded. Children died all the time in the tenements. Eight families, fifty-two people, lived in 19 Railway Street, and every family had lost at least one baby or child.

"Your father stopped drinking just before we moved here. This was going to be our new start. But because he wasn't drinking, he didn't go into the pubs where the stevedores hire men for the docks. So he didn't find work as easily." Nan looked around the room. "We've been here eight years, we came here just before your brother was born. I thought I'd never leave this house in my lifetime. But now . . ." Her gaze drifted to the still figure on the bed.

The boy saw fear in her dull grey eyes, and knew she was thinking about eviction. Reaching over, he pressed her fingers wordlessly.

She covered his hand with her own. "You're a good lad, so you are. Go get your brother and sister; it's time for dinner."

There was a rat on the table.

The single room was dominated by the table. Once, long ago, it would have been beautiful, an oval of highly polished wood with a rope edge design and claw feet. But generations of misuse and abuse in an atmosphere of continual damp had warped and spread the boards, and the elegant feet were chipped and hacked into unrecognisable lumps. The table really was too big for the room, but, along with four mismatched chairs, a double bed for Nan and Frank, and a single mattress on the floor in the corner where the three children slept, there was no other furnishing in the room. Cooking was done over the open fire, and a single outhouse in the backyard served for the entire tenement.

At the sight of the rat, Mickser felt his stomach sour. He hated rats. He had a vivid memory of wakening as a child and finding a fat, musty-smelling rat crouched on his chest, yellow teeth and beady eyes less than an inch away from his face. His screams had awakened the entire house. He had screamed himself awake for months afterwards.

The stew had been placed on the centre of the table in a chipped blue bowl, waiting for Mickser to return with his brother and sister. There were four plates set out, with an assortment of spoons alongside them. The boy noted fleetingly that his plate was now in his father's customary position. Across the room, Nan sat on the side of the bed and spoon-fed her husband tiny pieces of meat and soup. Mickser's bare feet made no sound on the wooden floor as he entered. She didn't even glance up.

With its bright eyes fixed on Mickser, the rat rose on its hind legs and perched its front paws on the edge of the bowl. Its evil head dipped swiftly into the bowl and tugged out a huge chunk of meat. Clutching the meat firmly in its jaws, the rat turned and leaped onto a chair, then to the floor. Before the boy could react the creature had darted straight between his legs and down the stairs.

Mickser raced after it, rage and disgust lending him speed. He didn't stop to think what he would do if he caught up with the rat. But he had discovered the pawn tickets on the mantelpiece. He didn't know what his mother had pawned for the price of the dinner, he didn't know what she had left to pawn, but he certainly wasn't going to allow it to be stolen by a rat.

Down the stairs – brushing past his startled brother and sister, who were on the way up – Mickser's full attention was on the rat. It was as big as a small cat and he was sure he had seen it about before. The tenements were infested with vermin of all sorts, fleas, cockroaches and rats, especially rats. Last summer, the O'Neills' new baby had had its nose bitten off by a rat.

The rat ran toward the passage at the back of the house, claws clicking on the bare floor, tail slithering, the piece of meat in its jaws leaving a greasy trail in its wake. Abruptly it disappeared down the cellar stairs. Mickser hesitated a moment on the top stair. He hated going down into the cellar, which was so foul that the landlord could not rent it. The damp, squalid hole was infested with rats and fleas, the air almost unbreathable.

The rat's nails clicked mockingly as it ran down the stairs. But he would not let it escape, even if it meant facing the cellar. Drawing a deep breath, Mickser started down.

At the bottom of the steps was a row of arched openings. They looked as if they had once been fitted with doors, but the dampness must have rotted them away . . . or the inhabitants upstairs had chopped them up for firewood.

Mickser stopped on the last step and allowed his eyes to become accustomed to the gloom. When his thumping heartbeat had slowed and his ragged breathing had stilled, he became aware of the cellar noises. The constant rustling, rattling susurrations of something – many things – moving.

This was not such a good idea.

The boy eased down onto the cellar floor. He had only taken a couple of steps forward before he halted again with a gasp, his toes curling. Something furry had squirmed beneath the arch of his left foot. Carefully, he lifted his foot and stepped backwards.

A shroud-like cobweb promptly wrapped itself around his head.

Not a good idea at all.

Something rattled to his right, clinked and fell silent. Mickser backed away, stepping into a dark cubicle. His shoulder blades touched rotten shelves. With his eyes firmly fixed on the darkness in front of him, Mickser quested along the lowest of the shelves, looking for something he could throw. If he attracted the attention of whatever was in the cellar and it ran in the opposite direction, he would make a run for the stairs.

His fingers felt cobwebs as thick as a girl's hair. And just beyond – cool metal. Gratefully, Mickser wrapped his hand around a thin metal bar . . .

CHAPTER SIX

Sophie stood at the window and gazed down into the moonlit street below. "I wish I were dead," she said. But she did not mean it, she was merely trying on the words. She did not even know what dead meant, not really. Mama and Papa were dead, lying somewhere at the bottom of the sea. No matter how she tried she could not imagine them there, nor what it must be like for them.

Being dead.

In spite of the flannel dressing-gown she wore over her cambric nightdress, Sophie shuddered. Her bedchamber was cold. At sundown a chambermaid had come to light the fire, but the cheerful blaze had long since dwindled to a few glowing coals. They could not chase away the chill she felt inside. And she was hungry. Her stomach was growling in a way no lady's ever should.

Mademoiselle was always trying to make a

lady of her. Perhaps the hated governess had been ordered to prepare her to be Robert's wife. Was that it? Did he mean to marry her as soon as she was properly polished? Sometimes he looked at her in such a strange, speculative way . . .

The room seemed to be growing colder and the shadows in the corners were writhing into sinister shapes. Sophie had been unable to fall asleep in the big four-poster bed; she felt suffocated by its heavy draperies. What a cheerless place her bedchamber had become. Leaning on the windowsill, she addressed the friendly face of the moon. "I would not marry Cousin Robert if he had a thousand pounds," she said. "Not even a *million* pounds!" She had no clear idea of how much a thousand pounds might be, never mind a million. She just liked the drama of the words.

Cold wind slammed against the glass, forcing her to take a step backward. But there was no place warm and safe to go. If only she were still in the nursery!

Then Sophie had an inspiration. She would reclaim some of the treasures Cousin Robert had taken from the nursery. Hidden in her bedchamber, they would keep her company on nights like this when her loneliness and unhappiness became unbearable. Dearly loved items from a childhood fast retreating into memory could be secreted at the back of the wardrobe, or even in the bedside cabinet with her chamber pot. Mademoiselle would never find them. She was only interested in what she considered valuables.

Once she had the idea Sophie could not wait to act upon it. She wrapped her dressing-gown more snugly around herself and went to the door. The handle turned silently. A moment later she stood on the second-storey landing.

With her head cocked to one side, she listened intently. The house was quiet. Only the wind was awake, stalking around the walls outside, rattling windows and seeking entry. But 19 Mecklenburg Street was solidly built, not even a cold draught could enter.

So why am I so cold? wondered the girl as she tiptoed down the curving front staircase. In a cloakroom off the entrance hall was a green baize door that opened into a service passage lined with shelves and cupboards. Leading to the back stairs, the passage gave access to both the attic and the cellar.

It was a long climb to the attic. The cellar was much nearer, down only one flight of steps. Although the door to the cellar stair was fitted with a lock, Sophie was pleased to discover that it was open. Cousin Robert often went down there for a last bottle of port before retiring. He preferred to make his own selection rather than leave the choice to Garrett, and he was careless about locking up behind himself.

On a shelf beside the door was a small oil lamp with the wick set low. Mrs Mayne always kept some light burning in the service areas, in case the servants were needed during the night. Sophie turned up the wick until a warm yellow light filled the glass chimney. Then, holding the lamp aloft, she started down.

The stairs were steep, with only a narrow handrail on one side. The bare brick walls smelled of damp. In Mama's day, Mrs Mayne would have been ordered to scrub those walls twice a year with a carbolic solution. Now that Cousin Robert ran the house, standards were different. He only cared about what showed.

At the bottom of the steps was a row of unpainted timber doors. Each bore a small, neatly lettered sign: Buttery, Trunk Room, Tool Room, Coal. And one that read simply, Misc. Storage.

There was no lock on the storeroom door but the wood had warped, swelling in the frame. Opening it was difficult. Sophie set the lamp on the floor and tugged on the door handle with both hands. Nothing happened. She pulled harder. After a moment the door opened with a screech.

She picked up the lamp and stepped inside.

Shapes materialised from the darkness. Disused bits of furniture and garden equipment lay beside rolls of worn carpet. A battered brass birdcage, door ajar, mourned its missing canary. Propped in one corner was a wheelbarrow with its wheel missing. An old tin hip-bath held an assortment of worn cleaning brushes. Faded draperies which Mrs Mayne intended to make into something else someday were neatly stacked on wooden shelves, and . . .

. . . and . . .

Sophie gave a cry of delight. Protruding from one of the shelves was the handle of Nurse's dear old iron toasting fork! It was an omen, the first memory she would reclaim as her own.

Darting forward, she closed her fingers around the handle . . .

CHAPTER SEVEN

. . . just as another hand grasped it too.

The boy gave a cry of surprise and jumped back, but he did not turn loose of the metal bar. Never turn loose of anything valuable, that was his motto. Cobwebs plastered his face, veiling his eyes, clinging to his lips. Frantically he scraped them off . . .

And met the eyes of a red-haired girl not much older than himself. She was holding onto the other end of the metal bar, which he now recognised as a large, long-tined fork.

She was as startled as he was. "Who are you?" she demanded to know.

"Who are you?" he replied, fear making his voice harsh. "And what are you doing down here?"

"What am I doing here? You are the one with some explaining to do."

The girl's accent was a strange mixture of snob

and toff, but definitely Dublin. She was dressed like someone from an old-fashioned painting in a shop window, with a high-necked gown and some sort of coat over it.

Then, suddenly, shockingly, Mickser realised that he could make out the outline of the brick wall behind her. He was seeing the bricks through her body. She was almost, but not quite, transparent.

"You're a ghost!" Mickser dropped the fork to bless himself.

At the same moment the girl shrieked and also turned loose of the fork.

And disappeared.

Mickser stared at the space where she had been. He had seen a ghost. Everyone knew the tenements were haunted. But he had seen one. A ghost.

Probably a banshee.

Probably come to warn him about his father's death.

Then the shakes began, and Mickser felt his legs give way.

When Sophie released the fork the boy was gone as abruptly as a candle blown out. Yet she knew she had seen him, she could recall every detail of his shabby clothes and starveling face, the look of shock in his black eyes.

She had been able to see *through* him . . .

Through him!

As her heart began to pound with terror, Sophie realised that she had seen a ghost.

She wanted to run from the cellar and never come back. She would run to Cook and tell her, "I saw a ghost!" But then would Cook not send her to Mademoiselle?

Of course she would. And Mademoiselle would punish her for lying, or at the very least for having too much imagination. Mademoiselle did not believe young ladies should have imagination.

Sophie got as far as the foot of the stairs, then stopped and stood trembling, trying to think. "Perhaps no one was there at all," she told herself. "Perhaps it was only a trick of the light, a fragment of a dream . . ."

But she knew that this had been no dream. She had seen him so clearly! A poor thin boy – or a ghost of a poor thin boy – all alone in the dark.

As she was alone.

She drew a long, shaky breath and went back to the storage room. Holding the lamp high, she cautiously surveyed the debris. No one hid there, no ghost lurked in the corner. Before her was merely a jumble of discarded objects, the unwanted and unloved.

Then Sophie's eye fell on the toasting fork. Her newly found treasure.

She reached for the handle of the fork.

Mickser was used to being scared. There were a lot of things to fear in his life. He was afraid of the bigger boys in the street who beat him up; he was afraid of the way his belly felt when it cramped with hunger. He was afraid of stone bruises, those terrible boils that came up on bare feet. Most of all, he was afraid of his Daddy dying.

There were things that could hurt you, and things that couldn't. And ghosts couldn't. So there was no reason to be afraid of a ghost, he reasoned as he came shakily to his feet.

No reason.

His bare feet touched cool metal.

He was not going to give up a perfectly good piece of iron somebody might pay a ha'penny for, a ha'penny that could buy a bit of food for his Daddy.

Stooping, he grabbed the fork again.

He saw the hand first. Pale skin, translucent, perfect fingernails; a feminine right hand was wrapped around the other end of the fork. Mickser lifted his eyes . . .

She was there, staring at him, mouth open in amazement.

Instinct made him try to pull the fork from her grasp. "I saw it first!" he said defiantly. "So it's mine and you can't have it."

She shook her head. "It is mine. Nurse used to toast bread for me on this fork."

"Nurse? You don't look sick to me."

In spite of herself Sophie smiled. "Not that sort of nurse. I mean the woman who took care of me in the nursery."

Mickser tightened his grip on the fork. "Well this ain't your nursery. What I find down here is mine. Give it here!"

The girl's lips narrowed into a determined line. "No." With her left hand, she held up an oil lamp that shed a faint yellow light around him. She stared at him for a long moment by its glow, then put the lamp down again and took the fork handle in both hands and gave it a sharp tug.

"No!" Mickser reached out to push her away. His solid hand connected with her shoulder . . . and passed right through her flesh.

Sophie saw the gesture coming and flinched, bracing herself for the impact, but when he touched her she felt nothing.

Once again the children stared at one another.

"Are you dead?" Sophie asked in a whisper.

"No. I am not. Are you?"

"Certainly not! I am Sophie Marie Rutledge,

44

aged fifteen years – almost sixteen – and I live at 19 Princess Sophie Mecklenburg Street. We share the same name, the street and I," she added proudly. "Except the street was named for King George's wife and I was named for my Grandmama."

Mickser was fascinated by the way she spoke. Her accent was definitely Dublin, but very quaint and posh compared to his as he replied, "This is 19 Railway Street, and I live here. Me, Mickser Lawless. With my family."

"You live here?" The girl waved her arm around. "You cannot possibly, we would have known. One of the servants would have seen you and reported it."

The boy laughed scornfully. "Servants? In this place?"

"There has been a full staff here ever since my Papa built this house," she retorted.

"Your Papa built this house? When?"

"Shortly before he and Mama married in 1758, eighteen years ago. It was his wedding gift to her."

Mickser felt his jaw drop. He did the sums quickly. "That would make it 1776." He saw the girl nod. "But this is 1907!"

CHAPTER EIGHT

The boy turned and ran.

He didn't realise, until he was at the top of the stairs, heart pounding, stomach churning, that he was still holding the cold iron fork. He threw himself out into the hallway, then turned with his back to the wall, the fork held out before him like a sword, watching the door. He half expected to hear her come running up the stairs after him.

Could you hear a ghost run?

But she didn't come. No red-haired shape materialised out of the gloom.

The boy gave a whoop of triumph. When he told her the year was 1907 she had frozen with astonishment. His brief, hard life had already taught Mickser to make the most of any opportunity. He vaguely remembered wrenching the fork from her hand and fleeing . . .

"Who's making all that racket?"

Mickser jumped as the door behind him opened a crack. Pushing himself away from the wall, he turned to face the door in the passage opposite the cellar.

"Stop fidgeting. Who's out there?"

"It's me, Granny . . . Mickser Lawless."

The door creaked open and a tiny, wizened woman appeared. She was enveloped in layers of mismatched clothing, and hunched almost double over a gnarled blackthorn stick. She pushed the black shawl off her sparse grey hair and stared at Mickser through her right eye. Her left eye was opaque with cataracts.

"Was you making all that noise, Lawless?

"Sorry, Granny."

"Was you trigging in these halls?" the old woman demanded to know.

Mickser shook his head. Then, realising the old woman probably couldn't see that well, said, "No, Granny, I'd never go trigging on your door. Me Mam would kill me."

He didn't bother to explain to the old woman that you didn't go trigging in your own hallways. You found a tenement where no one knew you, then you started on the top floor and knocked on as many doors as possible. He knew boys who could get a whole house in an uproar and escape through the maze of alleyways, streets and yards that surrounded the houses. If you were inexperienced, or particularly cowardly, you only knocked on old people's doors. During the summer months, Granny Hayes was plagued by youngsters who would come in though the hall, knock on her door and then slip out into the yard.

"Someone banged on my door," she accused irritably, sidling up to Mickser.

"I hit off the wall," said the boy, trying to sound innocent. His eyes were beginning to water from the odour of cheap rum and snuff that enveloped the old woman. Everyone in the house – indeed, everyone in Railway Street – called her Granny, though she often said that she had no living relative. She was rumoured to be nearly ninety, a phenomenal age in the tenements where forty was considered a good age.

"I thought I saw something in the cellar," Mickser elaborated. Suddenly he realised that Granny Hayes, who had lived all her life in this house, in the room facing the cellar, would know if anything unusual ever occurred down there.

"What sort of something?" The old woman put her claw-like hand on Mickser's arm. Her fingers bit painfully. "Help me out onto the stoop."

Walking slowly, trying not to breathe in the stale odour that wafted from the old woman's clothes with every step she took, Mickser escorted her down the passage and through the front of the house to the front door. There wintry sunlight etched the design of the shattered fanlight onto the worn floor.

"Now, lad, what did you see? Tell old Granny Hayes."

"I thought I saw . . ." he hesitated.

Granny Hayes rummaged in one of her many skirts and produced a white clay pipe. Clamping it between the gaps in her teeth, she started sucking noisily.

"I was chasing a rat," Mickser began again. "It was enormous."

"You haven't seen big rats," the old woman chuckled. "Now when I was a girl, there were big rats. You'd see them as large as cats, racing around the yards, and up around the markets they'd be even bigger. I heard tell of a rat that took a baby once, lifted it right out of its cot . . ."

"I chased this rat into the cellar," Mickser interrupted, knowing that if he allowed the old woman to continue, she would never stop.

"Stupid thing to do. Those stairs are rotten with mould. You could have gone straight through them."

Mickser hadn't thought of that at the time. But portions of the tenements were always falling down, stairs giving way, ceilings collapsing, walls dissolving beneath the slimy green rot that ate away at everything.

"There's probably a rat's nest down there, under them steps," Granny Hayes continued, almost gleefully. "You could have gone straight into it. They'd have eaten you alive." She stopped, blinking hard as they stepped out of the shadowy front hallway into the sunlight.

Mickser helped her sit on the top step, then waited while she smoothed her skirts. Within moments, he knew, the other old women in Railway Street would have appeared and would join her. Someone would produce tobacco or snuff or a little stone jug of porter or whisky, and they would sit there for the rest of the day, and put the world to rights.

"I thought I saw a ghost down there," he said, determined to make her listen.

The old woman tilted her head back and looked up at him. He noticed that her clear eye was a bright, brilliant blue. Suddenly he wondered what she must have looked like in her youth. Beneath the incredible tapestry of wrinkles that patterned her face, her cheek bones were still high and proud, her chin strong, and although her hair was a dirty grey, her eyebrows were black. "This isn't a haunted house," Granny Hayes said.

Then she crossed herself.

Mickser sat on the step beside her with the metal fork resting across his knees. There was no shame in discussing ghosts; everyone knew they existed and that certain houses were either haunted or possessed by the devil.

Sucking on her pipe, Granny Hayes said slowly, "There's a house in Cumberland Street that's haunted something shocking. And another in Mark's Alley, and there's two houses in Engine Alley that have ghosts in them . . . but I've never heard of a ghost here."

"I saw a girl."

The old woman stiffened. "Not a banshee?" The banshee was known to haunt many Dublin tenements, and wail for a coming death.

Mickser clasped his arms around his grubby knees and gazed off down the street. Rows of identical tenements lined either side of the cobbled road, but with the sun shining on them, gilding the chipped and cracked façades, the broken windows, the wrecked fanlights over the door, Railway Street looked almost pretty. Until you looked at the people, at the poverty in their faces, the rags on their backs.

"I don't think it was a banshee," he said slowly. The mere word frightened him. If the girl was a banshee, did that mean that he was going to die, because he had seen her? Or had she come to claim his father?

Granny Hayes confided, "I saw the banshee once. I was back from visiting a woman in

Christchurch Place, and I'd cut through Werburgh Street when suddenly this old woman appeared before me. Oh, she was terrible looking, old, twisted, with long grey hair and a big hook nose on her. She was dressed in rags and her hair looked like cobwebs."

Mickser glanced sidelong at Granny Hayes, wondering if she realised she had just described someone very like herself.

The old woman went on, "She reached into her pocket and took out a comb and started to comb her hair. I was frozen to the spot, because I knew what she was then. She turned to look at me, and her eyes were blazing. I saw her raise her hand, and that's when God gave me the strength to turn and run. I knew what she was going to do. She was going to throw her comb at me. And if it hit me, I'd be stone dead!"

"Did she?" Mickser asked in a whisper.

"Do I look dead to you?" Granny Hayes demanded. "No, she didn't. But I learned later that a young man who lived in our street, eighteen years old and strong as a bull, was taken that same day. Oh, the banshee's a terrible woman. Terrible."

"The thing I saw in the cellar was a young girl," Mickser confided, "not an old woman at all. A pretty girl, with beautiful red hair. She acted surprised to see me." He lifted the iron fork off his knees and showed it to the old woman. "She seemed to want this."

Granny Hayes took the fork from him and held it up, squinting at it in the sunlight. "This is a toasting fork. You stick a piece of bread on one end and hold it over a fire." She passed it back to the boy. "It may have been special to her when she was alive; ghosts often come back to look for something they particularly loved in life. What are you going to do with it?"

"Sell it," Mickser said quickly. "If I clean it up and rub that rust off, I might get a ha'penny for it, maybe even a penny . . ." He stopped; the old woman was shaking her head.

"If you get rid of the fork, the ghost might never leave you. You could be haunted for the rest of your life. I knew a young man was tormented by a gho . . ."

"But it's only a bit of metal," protested the boy.

"It's your connection to the ghost. She probably has the same fork in her time. When you both touch it at once, you form the link. Best see what she wants first, before you go selling it," Granny Hayes advised.

Mickser slouched on the stoop. "I was hoping to make a ha'penny," he muttered.

Granny Hayes fumbled among her clothing, then pressed a large copper ha'penny into

Mickser's hand, followed by two pennies. "Be a good lad and go down to the shop and get me two pennyworth of tobacco for me pipe. Keep the ha'penny. So you don't have to sell the fork today," she added.

CHAPTER NINE

Robert Rutledge stood in front of the pier glass in his bedchamber and surveyed his image with satisfaction. He saw a handsome, ruddy man with a square chin and ginger-coloured whiskers. He stroked those whiskers with pride, making sure every hair was in place.

Annette said they made him look distinguished. Annette Moulin – Mademoiselle, as he always called her in front of others – had excellent taste, he thought. A pity that wretched Sophie had not absorbed more of her style. But soon his cousin's shortcomings would cease to bother him.

When he went out onto the landing, Robert could see Mademoiselle waiting for him at the foot of the stairs.

Tiny, dark, and elegant, Annette Moulin forced a bright smile as she watched him come down to her. Privately she thought him a very unattractive man. His face was too red and he had too much belly. But soon he would be rich; very, very rich.

She tilted her head and purred, "*Bon soir*, Robert."

"Not here," he said anxiously, hurrying down the last few steps. "Come into the library, we can talk there without being overheard."

Inside the book-lined room he closed the heavy double doors and thumbed the latch. "Now, my dear. Some sherry?"

Mademoiselle dropped her eyes demurely. "Whatever you wish, Robert."

"Roe-*behr*. I like the way you pronounce my name. A French accent is so refined."

Unlike you, my friend, thought Annette as she sipped her sherry. She observed that he had begun to sweat.

"How are you getting along with the girl?" he asked.

"She is difficult. Headstrong, spoiled. In France we do not give young ladies of her station the freedom you do here, they are not encouraged to speak their minds. Your Sophie actually dares to contradict me!" Her black eyes snapped with anger.

Looking at the Frenchwoman, Robert thought she might prove to be a bit of a handful herself. Spirited, like a hot-blooded horse. But he would rein her in soon enough, he knew how to manage the most mettlesome mare. Norman, the Rutledge coachman, frequently complained that Mr Robert returned his saddle horse to the stables with bloody spur marks along its sides. Robert sneered at such soft-headed sentimentality. Animals had no feelings, their only purpose was to serve man.

Rather like women, he thought, watching Annette over the rim of his glass.

"From now until Christmas I need you to keep Sophie very much under control," he told the governess. "If I have anyone coming to this house on business she is not to speak to them, do you understand? In fact it might be better if she is kept out of sight as much as possible."

"Does that mean you no longer wish her to go for an afternoon carriage drive?"

"I think we may dispense with that. After all, the weather is growing cooler. We would not want the dear little creature to come down with a chill now, would we?" Smiling at Annette, Robert stroked his ginger whiskers.

CHAPTER TEN

Mademoiselle became more strict than ever. "Tea," she insisted, "is at half past six, Sophie, and not one minute later. Such discipline is good for your character; I myself have great self-discipline. When luncheon is over you are to rest in your bedchamber from two to four. Resting is important for proper digestion. From four until teatime you are to perfect your needlepoint in the upstairs sewing room. I have chosen a pattern of marigold and convolvulus for the cushion covers you are working on, because they will heighten your sense of colour. You Irish have a very poor sense of colour."

"What about my carriage drive?" Sophie asked innocently. Suddenly she longed to be outside, even with Mademoiselle. The house which had always been her home had begun to make her uneasy. A phantom lurked here, the ghost of a ragged and starving boy.

The governess said, "Your cousin and I feel the weather has turned too cold for outdoor excursions. If you are to have a complexion like mine your skin must be protected. Cold air will chap your face."

"But the air is not too cold today," replied the girl. "The sun is shining brightly and . . ."

"How dare you argue with me!"

Sophie protested, "I am not arguing, I merely said . . ."

Mademoiselle put the back of one white hand to her forehead in a dramatic gesture. "What am I to do with you? How am I to make a lady out of such a rude child? A girl like you should be grateful for my efforts. Do you think I have to be here? *Non!* I could be at home in Marseilles among civilised people. Instead I am trying to teach you the social graces which will keep you from being an embarrassment to Monsieur Robert, and you thank me by defying me."

"I do not wish to be an embarrassment to Cousin Robert," the girl said truthfully. "But why is it so urgent that I learn these things? Is there . . . I mean, does he intend . . ." At that moment her nerve failed her. Sophie could not bring herself to mention her deepest fear – that Cousin Robert meant to marry her once she was trained to his satisfaction.

But there was no other explanation, she thought sadly. He, who so admired everything

French, wanted her made into a copy of Mademoiselle so he would have a French wife.

"Stop stammering," demanded the governess. "Your speech hurts my ears. You do not round your vowels properly, you do not roll your r's, you have a dreadful Dublin accent."

In spite of herself Sophie's temper flared. "And why not? I have lived all my life in Dublin."

"You impossible girl! How dare you speak like that to your betters!"

"You are not one of my 'betters'. You are just a governess hired to instruct me."

For a moment Sophie thought Mademoiselle would strike her. The Frenchwoman's face went white with anger and two hectic red spots appeared on her cheeks. "That is enough. It is time you learned some respect. Into the cellar with you. Some hours alone will give you time to reflect on your impertinence."

Sophie drew back. "Do not lock me in the cellar! Please, Mademoiselle!"

But her fear only fuelled the woman's determination. Catching Sophie by the wrist, she pulled the girl along. Her grip was far stronger than one would have thought, given her small stature. Sophie did not dare really fight back, but she pleaded all the way.

Her words fell on deaf ears. Mademoiselle only halted when they reached the cellar door.

Pursing her lips, she gazed thoughtfully at the small lamp on its shelf.

At once Sophie understood. "You must at least let me have some light, Mademoiselle."

"I must? I *must*? You are in no position to give me orders, young lady!" Opening the door, the governess shoved Sophie inside and slammed the door behind her. "I shall release you when you are ready to apologise to me and not before," Mademoiselle called through the panel. There was the sound of a key turning in the iron lock.

"I am going to tell Cousin Robert about this!"

The governess only laughed. "What good will that do? He has given me complete charge of you, I can do whatever I like. You would do well to remember that."

Sophie heard her heels tap away along the brick floor of the service passage. French heels, like the ones she insisted Sophie wear.

Then silence.

The girl began to tremble.

Her hand found the stair-rail and she made her way down, one cautious step at a time. She had no idea what she would do when she reached the bottom. Just sit, probably. And wait.

The cellar had not frightened her when she had a lamp in her hand. But she was frightened now.

Something scuttled off in the darkness like a rat running across the floor.

Sophie retreated a few steps, then sat down at the midpoint of the stair and drew up her feet. Soon she was hugging her knees for comfort. Mademoiselle said the cold was bad for her complexion, but there was a bitter chill in the cellar. She hated being cold. It was almost as bad as being afraid.

Yet what was there to be afraid of, really? How could there be a ghost in a house where no one had ever died? Mama and Papa had died at sea. And besides, thought Sophie, it would be rather comforting to see their ghosts, proof that some part of them still existed.

But the ragged boy in the storage room was a different matter. There was something strange about him, even for a ghost. Wait . . . had he not said he lived in 1907? Sophie did swift sums in her head. 1907 was 131 years in the future. So he could not be a ghost. Yet neither was he solid flesh and blood. His hand had passed right through her and she felt nothing.

Then Sophie remembered the toasting fork. The boy had been visible to her only when they were both touching the fork. When he pulled it away from her he disappeared.

She swallowed, hard, and stood up.

Perhaps her toasting fork was still in the cellar. If it was, she meant to have it. She simply would not fall victim to her own fears!

CHAPTER ELEVEN

"Daddy!"

Mickser stopped in the doorway, surprised to see his father out of the bed. He couldn't remember the last time he had seen his father on his feet.

Frank Lawless turned slowly, awkwardly, to face the boy. Mickser suddenly realised how thin he was. His hair was almost all gone now and, with the wan sunlight on his face, painting his features in light and shadow, it looked like a skull.

Mickser forced himself to smile. "Daddy. It's good to see you up, are you feeling better?"

Frank Lawless moved gingerly away from the window ledge and shuffled across the bare floorboards. With a white-knuckled grip he held on first to the end of the bed, then the back of a chair and the edge of the table. "I'm getting better, son," he said cheerfully. He sat down in the high-backed wooden chair, stifling a sigh of pain. "Where's your Mam?"

"Mad Alice isn't well, so Mam said she'd mind the stall."

"Means we'll have fish tonight," Frank smiled.

Mad Alice was a distant relation of Nan Lawless. She had a fish stall at the corner of Cole's Lane and Henry Street and whenever she wasn't well – which usually meant she had given birth to another baby – Nan would mind the stall. She wasn't paid for the work, but she got to take home any unsold fish at the end of the day.

"How many childer has Mad Alice got now?" Frank Lawless asked. In spite of his best efforts, his voice was faint and weary. He picked at a scattering of hard, stale crumbs on the table and popped them into his mouth.

Mickser did a quick calculation. "This will be her fourteenth."

"Fourteen little ones; God bless her. But she's lucky. Her old man works in Guinness's. Gets a good wage, and gets to bring home porter for the babbies. Gets free porter himself too," the man added, licking dry lips. He glanced over at the blackened kettle on the fire. "Is there any tea?"

"I'll make you some," Mickser said immediately. As he passed the table, he dropped the iron toasting fork onto it.

"Where did you get this?" asked his father, picking up the fork.

Mickser lifted the kettle and shook it. Water sloshed inside; at least he wouldn't have to go down to the yard to pump some more. "Found it in the cellar," he replied. "I thought it might be worth something."

"It's a handsome piece," Frank said. "Solid iron. Old too. Maybe with a bit of polishing, you'd get a ha'penny or two for it."

"Granny Hayes said it was a toasting fork."

Frank Lawless turned the metal fork towards the light, squinting hard as he tried to make out the details. "Could be."

After blowing on the embers in the fireplace, Mickser carefully fed the fire bits of turf and fragments of coal he had picked up off the street as he followed the coal drays. When the flames started to take hold he lifted the kettle onto the fire, then immediately added tea to the cold water. "How old do you think the fork is?" he asked his father casually.

"Hard to say. Could be fifty, maybe even a hundred years old. They're common enough, though. At one time – when these houses were owned by wealthy families – every home would have had a nice one like this."

Mickser sat at the table opposite his father.

"What do you mean, when these houses were owned by wealthy families?"

Frank Lawless leaned over and fondly ruffled his son's hair. "At one stage, son, this house, and all the other houses in the street, and all the streets around here, would have been owned by some of the wealthiest people in Dublin. This room," he waved his arm around, "would probably have been a bedroom for just one person. Can you imagine? Or it might have been a study, with the walls lined with books and a big desk in the centre of the room."

"When was this, Daddy?" Mickser knew his father had always been interested in history.

"Oh, about a hundred years ago. You see, son, in 1801, the Act of Union was passed, the Irish Parliament was dissolved and Ireland became part of the United Kingdom. It was supposed to be for the good of the country . . . but it didn't really work. Many of the people who owned houses like these – and most would have been English – returned to England and left the houses in care of their agents. Do you know," he added, "I remember reading that you could buy a house like this for eight thousand pounds in 1790. Fifty years later, you were lucky if you got five hundred pounds for it."

The kettle began hissing, and Mickser returned to the fire. Wrapping a cloth around the handle, he lifted the heavy kettle off the fire and poured some of the thick black liquid into his father's tin mug. Returning the kettle to the fire, where it would simmer and stew for the rest of the day, he carried the mug back to the table. "There's no milk," he lamented.

"Not to worry," Frank Lawless said quietly, "you know I prefer it without milk."

Mickser nodded, but he knew it was a lie. His father loved milk and sometimes spoke wistfully of cream; an impossible luxury to the Lawless family.

"These houses were all bought up by greedy landlords," the man went on, "and then let on a room-by-room basis. Where once a single family with servants would have lived, now fifty, sixty or even seventy people lived. It's not too bad here," he said as he sipped the scalding black tea, "but there's places in the Liberties where you might find a hundred people living in a house built for one family."

Frank coughed, the sound soft and wet, then hastily wiped his lips on his sleeve before his son could see the bloody froth. "The landlords packed the people in, renting every little space from cellar to attic where they could. And of course they never did any repairs. Why, only five years ago, a tenement collapsed in Townsend Street and wiped out two whole families." He shook his head and coughed again. "Isn't it strange to think that these were once the dwellings of the wealthiest people in Dublin . . . in all of Ireland. What would they say if they could see their houses now?"

A sudden bout of coughing bent him double. Mickser bit the inside of his cheek as the agonised, liquid rattle went on and on. This time Frank couldn't hide the blood on his lips. "I think I'll go and lie down for bit," he whispered.

Mickser came around and stood behind his father, helping him to his feet. "I'm sure I'm getting stronger," his father said with false confidence. "Be up and about in no time. You'll see. As soon as spring comes I'll be my old self."

"Yes, Daddy."

The boy helped his father into bed, pulled the blankets and coats up to his chin and then returned to the table for the tea cup. He drew a chair over alongside the bed and placed the cup on it, in easy reach.

"You're a good lad, Mickser. The best."

The boy nodded, unwilling to trust his voice.

"Lying here, looking up all the time, I finally got to look at the ceiling. Have you ever *looked* at the ceiling, Mickser?"

The boy dutifully looked up. Perhaps the ceiling had once been white. But now it was grey, lined with cracks, with thick mossy cobwebs in the corners and a green-rimmed stain slowly spreading toward the centre of the ceiling. There was a hole in one corner, which his father had once stuffed with newspapers to keep the rats and cockroaches from dropping into the room.

"Do you see that plasterwork?" his father asked.

In one corner of the ceiling clung the ragged remains of the decorative plasterwork that once ran around the entire ceiling. Mickser saw what looked like bunches of grapes and vine leaves. "I've never really looked at it before," he admitted.

"These must have been beautiful houses, Mickser."

The boy laughed sourly. "It's hard to think of any house on Railway Street being beautiful."

"Oh, but it wouldn't have been Railway Street then, Mickser. When the houses on this street were very grand, it had a very grand name: Princess Sophie Mecklenburg Street."

CHAPTER TWELVE

Sophie felt her way carefully along the wall,
searching for the room labelled Misc. Storage. It
was on the right-hand side, she recalled, and she
had left the door ajar.

Yes, here it was. Her nose recognised that
dusty, musty smell, compounded of neglected
wood and dusty fabric. She hesitated outside the
doorway, surprised to note the faintest glow
coming from inside. In that dark cellar it shone
out like a beacon.

"Is anyone there?" Sophie called cautiously.

There was no answer. The light continued to
shine.

Mystified, she put her head round the door
and peered in.

The stub of a candle was floating in mid-air.

Sophie gasped.

The candle swooped downward as if someone

had almost dropped it, then steadied again. By its glow Sophie could just make out a dim shape, or the effect of light on that shape. She found herself staring at a long, thin object, with two prongs at the end . . .

"My toasting fork!" she cried with delight. But as her fingers closed over the iron prongs, a hand appeared at the other end of the fork, clutching the handle. Sophie watched in astonishment while a figure materialised from the shadows: the ragged boy of the previous encounter.

This time she was careful not to let go of the fork. "Mickser, is it?" Her mouth was dry and her voice shaky.

The boy instinctively flinched, then straightened again and met her with a level look. "I forgot your name." He seemed to be having trouble with his voice, too.

"Sophie. Sophie Rutledge."

"You're the ghost, right?"

"I do not *think* so. I certainly am not dead. At least . . . not that I know," she added.

"Well, I think you are," the boy said flatly. "Anyone I can see through has got to be a ghost. And I can see right through you."

"But I can see through you. Does that not make you a ghost?"

The boy was silent, thinking. Then he ran his gaze around the storeroom. "What are you doing

71

down here, anyway? Why are you haunting a cellar?"

"I am not haunting this cellar, and I am most certainly not here by choice. I was locked in this disgusting place as a punishment." Feeling anger build in her all over again, Sophie explained about Mademoiselle locking her in the cellar.

As he listened to the girl, Mickser's eyes grew wider and wider. She was almost speaking a foreign language, a language which contained words he did not know, such as "governess" and "impertinence". When she finished her explanation, he replied, "I don't think I like that woman. That Mama-zelle, she lives in the house with you?"

Sophie nodded.

"Is she like a schoolteacher, this Mama-zelle?"

The ghost-girl smiled. "Something like, yes."

"You have a teacher living with you! Not sure I'd like that at all. But I wouldn't take no grief from her if I was you."

"Do you not obey your teachers, Mickser?"

The boy shrugged. "I suppose I did – when I went to school. But I don't go to school any more. Me Daddy has some education, but I guess I've had all I'm going to get. When Daddy took ill, I left school so I could help support the family."

"But you are just a child!"

"I'm old enough to work, to earn a few ha'pennies." Mickser's eyes ran swiftly over Sophie. "Hunh, I'm as old as you, I 'spect. I'm just small for me age. But I'm wiry." The boy let go of the fork and lifted his right arm, bending it at the elbow in order to make a muscle in his arm to show her.

The girl disappeared.

Mickser reached out and grabbed the metal fork again . . . and at once Sophie was standing before him. "I think we must both hold the fork if we are to see each other," she told him. "I wonder why?"

"Granny Hayes told me it was because it was special to you, and that you had come back to claim it," Mickser said. "She also said it was some sort of link."

"I think she must be correct. She sounds very wise, this Granny Hayes. Is she a relative of yours?"

"No. She's just an old woman who lives at the top of the cellar stairs."

Sophie frowned, trying to understand. In her house, the service passage was at the top of the stairs. The rooms opening off it were domestic offices such as the kitchen and the scullery. The only place a person could actually live in was the servants' hall.

"When will she let you out?" Mickser asked abruptly.

"Who?"

"Mama-zelle."

The girl half turned away from Mickser and gazed off into the gloom. "I don't know." She felt herself trembling. When she looked back at the boy, her eyes were huge and frightened in the light of his candle stub.

"I do not want to be alone down here," she admitted.

"Are you scared?"

"Would you not be frightened if you saw a ghost?" Sophie gave a nervous giggle. "But you think you *are* seeing a ghost. Me!"

"I'm not afraid of you."

"Nor I of you," the girl suddenly realised. "If you really are from 1907, which I find quite incredible, then I suppose you are not a ghost by definition. You are an apparition."

The boy scowled. "An appa . . . I'm not one of them, whatever you said."

"An apparition is like a vision, Mickser."

His frown gave way to a mischievous grin. "Like seeing a saint, you mean? I'm no saint, neither!"

Sophie's blue eyes twinkled. "Perhaps not. Anyway, I never heard of an apparition harming a person. But I must admit I am afraid of being locked down here alone. There are rats and spiders and mice in the dark." She gave a delicate shudder.

"Spiders and mice are all right . . . but rats now . . ." The boy shook his head. "I'm not sure I'd like to be spending the night down here on my own with the rats." He looked up the stairs, forehead creasing as he thought through an idea. "S'pose I can get you out?"

"Can you? How?"

"I know I can get myself out. There's no door at the top of the steps, all I have to do is climb up and walk out. I wonder . . . I wonder if you were to keep a good hold on that fork, would you be able to come out with me?"

"But then I would be . . . " Sophie hesitated. "I would be . . . where you come from."

"19 Railway Street," said Mickser. "You'd still be in your home. This street used to be called Princess Sophie Mecklenburg Street, just like you said. Maybe if I take you upstairs and let go of the fork, back in your own time you'll be outside the cellar."

The girl smiled at the ludicrous idea. Then the smile faded. She was talking to a ghost from the future; what could be more ludicrous than that?

"Let's try it," he urged. "Unless you got something better to do."

"Not at the moment." Sophie could feel her heart pounding. This was madness. She was making plans with an apparition. But if she did not go with him, what alternative was there?

Sit alone in the dark and listen to the rustling of the rats. Listen to them creep closer.

Drawing a deep breath, she tightened her grip on the toasting fork. "All right, Mickser," she said. "Lead on; take me with you."

CHAPTER THIRTEEN

Sophie listened for their footfalls on the gritty cellar floor, but she heard only one set of steps. Hers – or his?

She could not tell.

Holding tight to her end of the fork, she followed Mickser to the stairs.

The steps were like the ones in her own house. The cellar itself, she realised, was also much the same, except filthier. A servant hadn't been down here in months. But when they reached the top of the stair things were very different.

As Mickser had said, there was no cellar door.

A splintered doorframe opened into an unlighted passage. Mickser held his stub of candle to one side so the girl could see where she was going. As she stepped through the opening, her nostrils were assailed by a nauseating mix of odours: urine and faeces, rotting fruit and cabbage and the unmistakable stench of too many people crammed together in one place. Pressing her hand to her face, the girl pinched her nostrils closed and concentrated on breathing through her mouth. She regretted not having a pomander to hold in front of her face so the aromatic stuffing of the ball could mask the stench. Ladies and gentlemen frequently carried such pomanders when visiting odorous places.

Mickser, she noted, seemed unaffected by the smell.

Trying not to gag, she stepped forward.

The service passage down which Mademoiselle had – only moments ago, it seemed – dragged Sophie had been lined with shelves and cupboards. The passage Mickser led her into had the same proportions, but only a few fragments of plaster clung to otherwise bare brick walls.

The walls were stained with damp and mould partially concealed by flaking, dingy limewash. In places holes had been knocked in the surface, revealing wooden laths and decaying horsehair. She remembered her father telling her that the walls had been stuffed with horsehair to serve as insulation for the house. Filthy cobwebs sagged from the ceiling, heavily loaded with dust.

The cellar door had been opposite the door to the servants' hall in the house Sophie remembered. But there was no servants' hall here. From behind doors which should have opened into domestic offices came quarrelling voices and the sound of babies' crying.

"Where are we?" Sophie asked Mickser.

"I told you, my house. 19 Railway Street. Your house."

"This is like my house," Sophie admitted. "Only different. Ruined."

Mickser snorted. "Ruined! It's got a roof, windows, and all the rooms have doors. This isn't a ruin. I could show you places with no windows, the openings stuffed with papers, rags for doors. Now they are ruins."

The young couple were approaching the end of the passage. "Our room is up some more stairs," Mickser said. "We got to go to the front to get to it."

"You said room. How many of you live there?"

Mickser counted aloud, "Me Mam and Daddy, and me of course, then there's Thomas, he's eight and Emma, she's only four."

"Five of you in one room?" The girl was incredulous.

"That's nothing; the Redmonds on the floor above us have fifteen in one room. How many rooms do you live in?"

"Why, all of them. Except for the area belowstairs and the servants' quarters, that is."

"You're telling me you've a room all to yourself?" Mickser stopped and stared at her. He found the concept difficult to imagine.

"No, of course not."

The boy nodded to himself. He knew it couldn't be possible.

"There is my bedchamber of course, and a little sitting-room where I do my embroidery, and then there's my dressing-room. So I suppose I've really only the three rooms."

"Three rooms," repeated the boy numbly. "Where?"

As they emerged into the front hall, the girl tilted her head slightly and indicated the stairs. Young ladies did not point. "Up there, I think."

Slowly, the mismatched pair climbed the front staircase together. Sophie realised that she was trembling again, though not from fear. This was simply too unreal.

If she looked straight ahead she saw bare, warped wooden steps, with the centre worn down by the passage of countless feet. At the very edge of her vision, however, floated a gossamer image of the stairs as they were in her time, highly polished and gleaming.

They reached the first landing just as the door directly in front of them opened. Three of the Mulligan boys – the twins and Niall – came rushing out. Niall was carrying a loaf of bread like a football, tucked close to his chest.

"Hiya Mickser," he gasped, tearing off a ragged chunk of bread and tossing it at the boy as he leapt onto the first step . . . straight through Sophie.

The girl was too shocked even to scream.

Mickser too was speechless as he watched the red-headed twins run right through Sophie Rutledge as they chased their brother. When the footsteps had clattered all the way down the stairs and out into the street, he finally managed to say, "Didn't you feel anything?"

"Nothing," Sophie whispered. "I saw them run through me . . . yet I felt nothing. This is surely a dream."

"Well then we're both dreaming it," replied Mickser, "because I saw it too." He glanced sidelong at the girl, but she wasn't looking at him. She was staring through the open door in front of them.

Mickser glanced into the familiar room. Mrs Mulligan had her back to the door. The new baby was lying on the sagging bed, gurgling happily, while the woman changed its nappy, scraping its contents into the chamberpot at her feet. "Howya, Mrs Mulligan," Mickser called from the doorway.

"That you, Mickser?" the woman said without turning around. "How's your Da?"

"I think he's getting better," Mickser lied.

"I said a prayer for him at Mass this morning." Mrs Mulligan deftly wrapped a ragged cloth around the baby and pinned it closed. Then she picked up the child and rocked him gently in her arms while she shoved the chamberpot back beneath the bed with her foot.

"How's little Seán?" asked Mickser.

The woman tickled her baby beneath the chin, making him squeal with delight. "He's just grand. I thought he was getting a cold there last week, but I got some tallow and brown paper and stuck it on his back and he's in good form again. If you see those lads of mine down below, would you send them in to me? I need them to run a message."

"I'll do that," promised Mickser, backing out the open doorway. He stopped when he realised that Sophie wasn't moving. She was standing just inside the room, eyes and mouth wide, right hand pressed to her face. Mickser saw Mrs Mulligan looking at him then and gave the metal fork a warning tug. Reluctantly, Sophie turned away.

The girl suddenly stumbled and the boy reached out without thinking to catch her. His

82

hand passed through empty air. For a moment his stomach swooped within him.

"What's the matter with you?" he asked her when he could speak again.

Sophie gripped the banister rail so tightly he could actually see her knuckles change colour.

"That used to be my sitting-room," she replied faintly. "With my bedchamber beyond."

Sophie had gazed into a squalid tenement room with flaking walls and sagging ceiling, the only pieces of furniture two narrow metal-framed beds, an old door that was used as a table and three rickety chairs . . . but at the edges of her vision, she had caught glimpses of the room as it had been in her time.

As if wreathed in mist she had seen heavy flocked wallpaper, damask draperies, her favourite chair, her embroidery frame, the Persian carpet. And through an open doorway into the next room, her big four-poster bed with its curtains drawn . . .

"How many people sleep in that room?" she asked Mickser. Her voice sounded strained.

"Twelve."

"And do they eat there too?" She had noticed the fireplace was blackened, with pots sitting on the bare floor in front it.

"Eat, sleep, and do everything else there.

That's where they live; that's how they live. That's how we all live. In one room."

"I think I want to go back now," Sophie murmured. Her head was swimming. So many dreadful images, so many disturbing impressions, she feared if she remained any longer in this appalling place, she would scream.

"I can let go of the fork here . . ." Mickser began.

"No!" Sophie said quickly, "take me back to the cellar. That seems to have changed the least. Return me there; at least I shall know where I am."

They walked back down the stairs in silence. Sophie kept her head lowered, concentrating on the floor beneath her kidskin slippers. The floor of the front hall kept flickering between splintery bare boards and polished marble.

Once they had reached the cellar, Mickser turned to face the girl. "Will you be back?" he asked hopefully.

Until that moment Sophie would have answered, No, I never want to see this place again.

But she wanted to see him again. "Yes," she said slowly. "I suppose I can come back."

"What day is it in your time?"

"Tuesday."

"Same here. Why don't you come back to the

cellar on Thursday? First thing in the morning, 'fore it's hardly even light. I'll be waiting for you at the bottom of the stairs."

"I shall be here," Sophie agreed as she let go of her end of the fork . . . and abruptly winked out of existence, leaving Mickser holding the metal fork. The boy sighed and touched the tines she had been holding. He imagined they were still warm. There was a lingering trace of perfume in the air, like violets.

But he knew the girl wouldn't be back; he had seen the look of terror and disgust on her face as she had stared into the rooms which had once been hers.

CHAPTER FOURTEEN

"He is dangerously malnourished, Mrs Lawless."

Mickser pushed open the door and stepped into the room. The black-coated doctor was standing at his father's bed, carefully returning instruments to his bag. Frank Lawless seemed to be sleeping, but Mickser could see where his pillow was dark with blood.

Nan Lawless was standing at the head of the bed, hovering protectively over her husband. Her desperate eyes were fixed on the doctor's face.

"I know this is difficult for you, Mrs Lawless, but is there any way you could get him out into the countryside? The latest research from the Continent, particularly Switzerland, has shown that people with your husband's condition benefit remarkably from fresh clean air and a wholesome atmosphere. I would also recommend more meat in his diet. I realise that this is very difficult for you, of course."

"Very difficult," Nan Lawless repeated, without a trace of sarcasm.

The doctor, a young man with florid cheeks and a tiny pair of gold-rimmed glasses perched on the end of his nose, sighed. "There really is very little point in me returning, Mrs Lawless. You cannot move this man to a better environment; you are unable to provide him with a nourishing diet and you cannot afford any medication. I fail to see what I can do for him."

"You're perfectly right, doctor," replied Nan, her voice hard. "I was wrong to think that you could help. Well, rest assured that I will not be calling upon you again."

The young doctor opened his mouth to protest, but the look in the woman's eyes warned him. "I'll leave you this prescription," he said quietly, "just in case you do manage to get a few pennies."

"I'll find them," Nan Lawless promised.

Silently, the boy standing in the doorway echoed her words.

CHAPTER FIFTEEN

A subdued Sophie appeared at the breakfast table the morning after her experience in the cellar. Cousin Robert was in the dining-room when she entered, but Mademoiselle had not yet come down. Going to the polished mahogany sideboard, Sophie lifted the silver covers off the various chafing-dishes and gazed without enthusiasm at fluffy scrambled eggs, sizzling sausages, kidneys floating in cream. She settled for one of Cook's fruit scones and a cup of tea.

Cousin Robert glanced at her plate as she sat down. "Is that all you want?"

Sophie kept her eyes lowered. "Mademoiselle says a lady should have a dainty appetite."

"I am pleased to see you taking her advice. I never knew a child could eat as much as you do; food costs money, you know."

Sophie nibbled the scone without replying. After observing life in 19 Railway Street, she was ashamed of the amount of food piled on the sideboard. Even after Cousin Robert had filled his plate several times, most of it would be returned to the kitchens untouched. The Lawless family could have survived for a week on that one meal.

Her guardian cleared his throat. "Mademoiselle tells me you were bold yesterday and she had to reprimand you. It seems to have done you some good, I must say."

Wordlessly, Sophie sipped her tea.

"She only does these things for your own good," Cousin Robert went on.

Sophie recalled crouching at the foot of the cellar stairs as Mademoiselle opened the door. She heard again the woman's gloating voice, calling, "Are you ready to apologise, or shall I leave you there all night? Your cousin will not mind, I can do whatever I like."

Mademoiselle had seemed almost disappointed when Sophie meekly replied, "I apologise." In spite of the apology, which she forced the girl to repeat several times, the governess had decreed that Sophie spend the rest of the day in her bedchamber.

She had not slept much that night. Her thoughts had chased one another like red squirrels playing in the trees, and they were all of the house, Number 19 Railway Street . . .

Number 19 Princess Sophie Mecklenburg Street
... then and now ... now and some future then.

When morning finally arrived and she was
allowed to come down for breakfast, Sophie was
still preoccupied. Her eyes took in the details of
her home as never before.

Now as she nibbled her scone, she put the
pieces of the puzzle together in her head.

There could be no doubt. This was the house
that would become 19 Railway Street. By 1907
the spacious rooms would be carved up into a
number of cramped, dilapidated flats, but it was
the same house.

Sophie grieved for the destruction of her
home; for the loss of the world she knew. Did
things always change so much, and so suddenly?
Was nothing certain, nothing permanent?

Cousin Robert's voice cut sharply through her
reverie. "I said – are you listening to me,
Sophie?"

She hastily swallowed a bite of scone and
almost choked. "I am listening," she managed to
whisper.

"Very well. I am planning something quite
nice for you and I expect a little appreciation. As
you know, your sixteenth birthday takes place
next Tuesday on Christmas Eve, so I thought we
should have a party here for you to celebrate."

"A party?" Sophie opened her eyes very wide.

Since Cousin Robert moved in there had been few visitors. He did not encourage them. The only people who came to see him were unsavoury-looking men with sharp eyes, who spoke to him in the library behind locked doors. After each of these visits he was always short-tempered.

A party would mean friends, laughter, a return of the happy times that had prevailed when Mama and Papa were alive. Sophie was overjoyed. "Can I ask anyone I like?"

"You may within reason," he replied. "But we have only a little time to prepare, so I suggest you draw up a list. Mademoiselle will advise you as to which guests are appropriate."

She will not, Sophie promised herself. It is my birthday and my party, and the less Mademoiselle has to do with it, the better.

She did discuss the party with Cook, however. As she sat in the warm kitchen inhaling the aroma of mutton roasting in the oven, Sophie remarked, "Perhaps Cousin Robert is beginning to like me after all."

Cook smiled at her. "Who could not help liking you, child?"

"I never thought he did. But surely he would not give a party for me unless he was fond of me. And oh Cook, I am looking forward to it! I shall invite Clara and Louise Maunsel and their brother James, and the Gardiner girls – all the dear friends I so rarely see these days. I want this house to come to life again. Everything has been so dreary since . . ." She sighed, then lifted her chin resolutely. "It's going to be better now, though. I shall make it so."

That night as the servants had their tea, Cook said to Garrett, "At least Sophie is going to have her party. Bless the child, perhaps Mr Robert really is fond of her."

Garrett took off his wire-rimmed spectacles and rubbed the bridge of his nose. "I would not be so quick to credit him with the milk of human kindness if I were you. I suspect the party is simply his effort to get into her good books. Remember that she will wake up on Christmas morning an heiress. This house and everything in it that Mr Robert is holding in trust will pass to her. Mr Robert will be left with nothing; she could evict him with a word . . . and there's nothing he could do about it."

"Pass me some more of the blackcurrant jelly," Cook requested. "It came out very well this year, if I do say so myself. Och, Garrett, Miss Sophie will never evict Mr Robert. The girl is too kind-hearted, in spite of her redheaded temper. Can you picture her casting her nearest living relative out in the cold? Though it might serve him right if she did. If you ask me, he and that Frenchwoman of his are . . ."

Just then Garrett shot a glance down the table toward Mrs Maynes. The housekeeper, who had grown exceedingly deaf, was leaning forward and looking in their direction. Garrett caught Cook's eye and gave a tiny shake of his head to warn her to change the subject.

As the butler knew, Mrs Maynes had transferred her loyalties without question to the person who paid her. Until Christmas Eve, less than a week away now, Robert Rutledge controlled the purse-strings.

What would happen after that was anyone's guess.

CHAPTER SIXTEEN

On Thursday morning Sophie awoke very early. The pale light of a grey dawn was seeping into the room. An icy breeze blew through the open window, reminding her of the passage of time. Less than a week to Christmas.

Shivering, she got out of bed and padded over to close the window. She hated the cold. Eventually the chambermaid would come bustling in to light a fire so she could dress in comfort. But Sophie must not return to her warm bed, not this morning. She had an appointment to keep.

What sort of a morning was it for Mickser, she wondered. Was he cold? Was he hungry?

She dressed hastily and wrapped a woollen shawl around her shoulders. Then she groped under the feather bed on her four-poster until she found the toasting fork. Concealing it in the folds of her shawl, she passed out through her sitting-room and onto the landing.

Shadows still carpeted the main staircase. But the fanlight over the front door provided enough illumination to make the crystal prisms on the chandelier glitter like ice.

At the door to the cellar Sophie hesitated as a cold draught swirled around her ankles. Then, biting her lip, she opened the door and stepped into the darkness. Each step creaked and sighed as she stood on it. Standing on the last step, she paused.

"Mickser?"

She held the fork by the tines and waved the handle slowly back and forth in empty space.

"Mickser . . ."

With every wave she felt more foolish. There was no one there, this was all her imagina . . .

Something caught hold of the other end of the fork and held on tight.

A moment later Mickser Lawless stood before her. "So you did come," he said. He wore the same ragged clothes as before, and his face was, if anything, even thinner. But his eyes were bright and he seemed genuinely happy to see her.

"You sound surprised," she whispered.

"I suppose I am," he admitted. "Why did you come here?"

"Curiosity," she said. "And you?"

"Curiosity."

Together they climbed the stairs. There was no one in the service passage. The house was still quiet. Soon, however, Mrs Maynes would be dispatching the maids to their duties and Cook would be busy preparing breakfast, while Garrett went to take his day's instruction from Robert Rutledge. Sophie turned to Mickser, but he was gazing past her down the passage. "What's all them boxes on the walls? Some of them have padlocks, even."

"They are cupboards to hold things we are not using."

The boy struggled to comprehend a family with more material goods than they could use.

"You're seeing *my* house," Sophie told him, delighted with the realisation.

Mickser blinked in amazement. He was actually looking into Sophie's time, whereas before she had been looking into his.

"It must be because I brought the fork this time," Sophie said. "Last time, you brought the fork."

He nodded. "That must be it. So does this mean I get to see how you live now?"

"I do not know," admitted the girl, "but we shall soon find out. Come on."

As Sophie started off down the passage

Mickser stayed close to her, being careful to keep his hand on the iron fork.

At that moment Garrett, smoothing his hair back with his palms and yawning hugely, emerged from the servants' hall and halted in surprise. "Miss Sophie, what are you doing down here?" Although Mickser was standing less than a foot away from her, the servant was unable to see him.

"I could not sleep," she replied. "I was . . . looking for Cook."

His face softened with pity. "You poor mite, you miss not having a mother. But it is chilly here, you should go back to your warm bed. Mrs Maynes can send a chambermaid to you with a warming pan."

"Perhaps later, Garrett." Sophie continued down the passage and out through the green baize door with Mickser at her heels.

"Who was that?" the boy asked under his breath.

"Garrett. Our butler."

"Butler." Mickser shook his head. King Edward VII and Queen Alexandra had butlers, or so he heard somewhere. But he had never even seen a butler before.

Sophie led him into the front hall, where he stopped and looked in wonderment from the gleaming marble floor to the elaborately ornamented ceiling with its wreaths and medallions of white stucco. "That plasterwork is by Edward Semple, the famous *stuccodore*," Sophie explained, as if the name could mean anything to the boy. He recalled the decayed fragments his father had pointed out to him on their own ceiling; so this was what such things had looked like when they were new and whole!

Though the shape and size of the hallway were familiar to him, everything else was strange, a revelation. Yet at the very corner of his vision he could see where the beautiful plasterwork dissolved into a rotten ruin; where the black and white marble floor disintegrated into bare boards spongy with dry rot.

Mickser looked up wide-eyed at the chandelier above the polished rosewood table in the centre of the hall. "Does that never fall down? If it did, you could prob'ly sell them sparkly bits."

"What funny ideas you have, Mickser! That is antique French crystal."

Mickser nodded, though he had no idea what antique French crystal was.

On one wall was a large mirror in a golden frame. When Sophie paused in front of the glass, Mickser gazed over her shoulder. Initially there was only one image in the glass, then slowly, almost imperceptibly, both reflections appeared side by side. He saw a pretty girl with coppery curls and a firm, square chin; she saw a grave, gaunt lad whom poverty would make a man before his time. But as their eyes met there was a smile on his lips – and hers.

Abruptly Mademoiselle appeared at the top of the stairs and clapped her hands. "Sophie! What are you doing out of your room so early? Return to your bed at once."

Startled, Mickser dropped his end of the toasting fork.

Ignoring the governess, Sophie whirled around looking for Mickser, but the boy had vanished. The link between them had been broken and she could no longer see him, a boy out of his time. "Mickser," she whispered urgently.

"What did you say? What did you say?" snapped Mademoiselle.

"Nothing, Mademoiselle," the girl replied.

"Return to your room – now! Or else! You know what happens when you are impertinent."

Mickser stared after Sophie as she hurried up the stairs. He was astonished that he could still see her. Then he realised he had somehow become trapped in 19 Mecklenburg Street. His eyes followed Sophie until she reached the first landing. Then, snapping out of his trance, he hurried after her, only to discover that the walls around him had become curiously blurred.

Simultaneously he was surrounded by the entrance hall of Sophie's home and the filthy front passage of 19 Railway Street. All definition between them was gone. One lay over, or under, the other.

The effect made his stomach lurch.

Mickser rubbed his eyes and ran up the stairs after Sophie, only to become hopelessly confused.

He found himself wandering in and out of chambers that were as insubstantial as fog. Sculptured chimney pieces of snowy white marble reached halfway to the high ceilings. Colourful Turkish carpets on the floors and heavy crimson draperies of satin damask at the windows muffled sound. Yet beneath all this, like objects seen underwater, were blocked and broken fireplaces, filthy bare floors, smashed windows patched with bits of timber, stuffed with paper. In some, he could see the people of his time, moving like smoke wraiths around the rooms, unaware that they were living their squalid lives amidst the luxury.

Mickser was increasingly frightened. What if he was trapped forever in this in-between place, in neither one world nor the other? Who would help Mam with Daddy and the children? He had to find Sophie. He tried to remember what Sophie had said about her bedchamber. It had been on the first floor, in the Mulligan's room . . .

all he had to do was to find the Mulligan's room. He was sure it was on this floor . . . but where?

"Sophie!" he called desperately.

From behind a half-closed door a woman's startled voice cried out, "What was that?"

Mickser froze. It was the woman at the head of the stairs; the one Sophie had gone running to. Mama-zelle.

A man answered, "Wind wailing down the chimney; it can create very strange effects. Annette, you must control your nerves."

"My nerves are steel, you need have no fear. I was simply concerned that someone might have overheard us." The door opened suddenly and the sharp-faced governess looked out, staring straight at Mickser. She looked up and down the hall before closing the door again. The boy heard the lock click shut. "I never helped plan a murder before."

"You are very good at it for an amateur," he replied sarcastically. "Are you certain we can get away with it?"

"Of course we can," said the woman. "You have to be resolute."

"I am."

"Good. Even the weather is on our side. This will work; trust me."

"Oh, I do. I do. A man should always trust his future wife."

101

Mickser was horrified. The boy was about to push through the door when he heard his name called.

"Mickser?"

"Did you hear that this time!" Mama-zelle demanded to know.

"I heard nothing, Annette. What is wrong with you?"

"Mickser . . . where are you?" Sophie wailed from someplace else in the house.

The boy turned and fled back down the stairs before the dreadful Frenchwoman could emerge from the room and catch the girl again.

CHAPTER SEVENTEEN

There.

The metal fork.

The morning light seeping through the fanlight – broken and cobwebbed in his time, whole and sparkling in hers – glinted on metal. Mickser ran straight towards it, reaching for it as a drowning man grabs for a float. One of the sharp tines grazed his hand but he did not care, he had hold of the fork once more.

Sophie appeared, her worried eyes gazed into his. "I was afraid I might not find you again."

"*You* was afraid!"

"Mademoiselle made me give her the fork, but I saw where she put it. As soon as she was busy elsewhere I retrieved it and came looking for you."

"Take me back to the cellar, quick," said the boy in a shaken voice.

"What is the matter?"

"Our two houses . . . I saw . . . I can't explain. When I hadn't got hold of the fork, I saw both houses at the same time, one picture over another . . . it was . . . terrifying. I didn't know where I was. I wasn't sure when I was. I want to go home, Sophie, to my time. And I think the only way into my time from yours is the cellar because it hasn't changed much. The rest of this house is too . . ." He struggled for words, "too . . . different."

She did not understand, but his distress was obvious. So with Mickser grasping the fork in a white-knuckled grip, Sophie led the way back to the cellar door.

This time they saw no one. Before opening the door it was her turn to ask, "Shall we meet again?"

He did not want this girl to know how frightened he really had been. And he did want to see her again, though he could not have said why. What was happening between them was scary but it was also exciting. "Fair enough. Tomorrow . . . ?"

"Tomorrow is Friday. I am not sure I would be able to see you tomorrow. Mademoiselle has said the dressmaker is coming to fit some new frocks. It is my birthday next Tuesday, Christmas Eve, and there is to be a party."

Mickser didn't know when his birthday was, and he'd never had a party.

"Fair enough," Mickser said hurriedly, "not tomorrow. Make it Saturday then. I'll meet you in the cellar at the same time."

"I shall be there," Sophie began to promise, but Mickser had already turned loose of the fork and vanished.

True to his word, two days later he was waiting in the cellar with the fork in his hand when he felt someone touch it. Moments later, Sophie Rutledge flowed into existence, her hand closed over the handle of the toasting fork. He grinned at her. "This is my fork in my time . . . so welcome to my world. Are you ready?"

Sophie's mouth was dry but she refused to be afraid. "I am ready."

"Come on, then." Mickser turned and went back up the cellar steps with Sophie close behind him.

The door at the top of the stairs was gone. Sophie knew she was back in the poverty-stricken Dublin of 1907.

"What do you want to do first?" inquired Mickser.

"I should like to see outside," the girl said, "but before that . . . would you show me where you live?" she asked almost shyly.

Mickser shrugged. "Won't be anything like you're used to. But come on then."

He led Sophie up the front stairs to the landing. There the girl stopped for a moment, looking down a hallway she once knew so well, but which was now almost unrecognisable. In her time there were portraits on the walls and peacock feathers in tall China import vases. Candles had burned in brass sconces, creating a warm golden glow. Now, there was only darkness and dinginess and squalor.

"We're on the next floor up," Mickser told her. As he crossed a patch of bright new floorboards, he explained, "These were replaced a couple of weeks ago." He jerked his thumb at the closed door beyond the new boards. "Mr Mulvaney came out of his door one day and went straight through the floor." He grinned. "You should have heard him swear. He was stuck in it up to his waist, his feet dangling through the ceiling below."

Though the idea of someone crashing through rotting floorboards dismayed Sophie, she had to smile at the image.

The next floor was, if anything, even darker than the first. Sophie wondered if the rents got cheaper the higher you went in the house. Mickser led her to the first door they came to, pushed it open and stepped inside. Sophie remembered this room. It had been a guest bedchamber called the Blue Room because it was decorated in cool shades of blue and ivory.

Now nothing of either colour remained.

An old, haggard woman was sitting on the edge of a filthy bed, spoon-feeding watery soup to an equally old man. When the woman looked up, Sophie revised her estimate of her age. She also recognised her resemblance to the boy.

"Hiya, Mam."

"You're back early, Mickser," Nan Lawless said. "I was just giving your Daddy his breakfast."

"I just came back to see if there was anything you wanted me to do for you."

The woman gave a tired sigh. "Nothing at all, Mickser. We're grand."

Sophie's heart throbbed with pity as she looked at Mickser's father. She did not know his true age, but he looked ancient. He skin was wrinkled like old leather and hung in folds beneath his chin and in deep black bags beneath his eyes. She had never seen flesh so yellow.

It was a few moments before she realised that the brown stain on the pillow and across the old man's cheek was dried blood.

Her eyes moved on to discover there was no furniture of any consequence, no comfort for the inhabitants. One broken table was the focus of the room. The adults slept in the only bed, the children slept on a mattress on the floor, meals were cooked over the open fire. The Lawless family would live and die in this single room.

"Are you still carrying that old fork, Mickser?" his mother asked.

He quickly explained, "I just want to clean it up before I sell it."

Moments later, Mickser turned and left the room, followed by a silent Sophie. She did not speak until they were standing at the hall door. "I wish there was something I could do."

"There's nothing anyone can do," Mickser replied, unable to keep the bitterness from his voice.

"But surely there must be something!"

"What? You live 130 years ago. Come see what it's like here now."

Stepping out onto the street was, for Sophie, like stepping into a nightmare. The handsome street she remembered, clean and bright and prosperous, was now lined with fetid tenements. Later, Sophie would recall that journey into twentieth-century Dublin as a series of images and impressions that would haunt the rest of her days. Strange-familiar streets . . . buildings without style or taste, buildings of a relentless drab ugliness . . . rubbish everywhere . . . and the people, the vast numbers of people! Unhappy-looking people with tense, anxious faces. People who coughed all the time, people whose eyes and noses streamed.

The air which had once been so clear was chokingly polluted with coal smoke.

As they walked through the city, Sophie observed to herself that everything was grim and grey. Where were the colours? Georgian Dublin with its red brick mansions had been replaced by endless rows of crowded tenements. Buildings that were new and elegant in Sophie's day were abandoned and dilapidated now. Houses she had visited, homes of friends she had known all her life, had been turned into smoke-blackened lodgings of the poorest sort. The lower floors of some had been made into shops whose windows displayed merchandise of dubious quality, in the worst possible taste.

The fashions were a scandal. Sophie even saw unaccompanied women walking in the streets. Men in long trousers rode about on strange wheeled monstrosities . . .

And the poor were everywhere . . .

There must have been poor in her own time, though she did not recall actually seeing any. Probably it was not allowed. Ladies were shielded from such sights.

But here the contrast was so sharp, so vivid. Her memories of her own time contrasted achingly with Mickser's world.

"I thought the world was supposed to advance, to move on," she said softly.

Mickser looked at her, nonplussed.

Sophie shook her head. "This world has not progressed . . . it has not progressed at all. People are worse off now than they were in my day. Take me back, Mickser," she said imperiously, "I do not like this place one bit."

"This is Dublin," Mickser said simply.

"It is not my Dublin. Next time, Mickser," she promised, "I will show you my Dublin."

CHAPTER EIGHTEEN

The morning had dawned bitterly cold, with occasional flurries of snow. The winter of 1776 was proving to be the worst Dublin had experienced for a very long time.

Mademoiselle stayed in bed with a chill. Sophie, who usually disliked winter, was delighted by the weather. She and Mickser would be able to leave the house without any interference from the governess.

Only Garrett saw his young mistress go out the front door carrying something half hidden in the folds of her fur-trimmed mantle. But he would not report her actions to Robert Rutledge.

And of course he could not see Sophie's companion at all.

As she set out to show Mickser the Dublin of her time, the girl said proudly, "This is *my* city. Papa called it the most beautiful capital in Europe."

"*Dublin — beautiful?*" Mickser echoed in disbelief.

"Just consider the buildings; the Rotunda, for example."

Approaching Rutland Square, the boy flicked a dismissive glance at the circular brick structure to which she referred. "That's not beautiful."

"Oh, Mickser, look again. The Rotunda was built by John Ensor in 1764 as a centrepiece for various pleasure-rooms to provide income for the Lying-In Hospital. Mama used to bring me to the tea room here on Sunday afternoons. I think the shape of the Rotunda is so elegant! The Hospital itself is similar in design to the Duke of Leinster's mansion on Kildare Street, you know. The architect Richard Cassels planned them both in the style of the great country houses."

Mickser raised his eyebrows. "What school did you go to? I never learnt none of that. Mind you," he added with a grin, "I didn't learn much of anything at school. Everything I know, I picked up off the streets."

"I was educated at home by tutors. Some of my friends like the Maunsel girls went away to school, but Mama and Papa wanted to keep me with them . . . " Her voice trembled with emotion. She closed her eyes for a moment, then said brightly, "Shall we walk down Sackville Street?

"The Wide Streets Commission is turning Dublin's narrow roads into thoroughfares," she went on. "Parliament Street was the first one they widened. When they are finished, this very Sackville Street will be the broadest, most beautiful boulevard in the British Isles." With a graceful gesture of her free arm, she indicated a breathtaking sweep of pavement.

Suddenly Mickser stopped. Careful not to let go of the iron fork, he looked up and down the street in both directions. Then he looked a second time as if he could not believe his eyes. This was a street he knew well . . . this was a street he walked day after day. "Where's the Pillar?"

"What Pillar?"

"Nelson's. Everybody knows the Pillar."

"Nelson who?" asked Sophie.

"I don't know exactly; some English man. The Pillar should be right there in the middle of the street, you can see it from every direction. But it's gone!"

"Perhaps it is not yet built," suggested the girl. Mickser looked so upset by the idea, however, that she changed the subject. "If you would like to go across the river we could view Trinity College. Neither you nor I shall attend there, of course; I am a female and you are poor. But the buildings are splendid."

A college seemed as remote to Mickser as the moon. "I don't need to see Trinity; I've see it often enough. Tell me about this place here instead," he said, pointing to an imposing mansion six bays wide. "I suppose you'd call that beautiful, would you?"

"I would. That is Drogheda House," replied Sophie, "the finest residence on Sackville Street. John Ensor built it too. The house was purchased five years ago by the Earl of Drogheda and is much admired. I love that round tower, and the parapet with the finials. Sometimes I pretend I am Princess Sophie Mecklenburg," she admitted in a whisper. "I imagine leaning out one of the tower windows as a prince comes galloping to carry me away."

Glancing at Sophie out of the corner of his eye, Mickser thought she looked rather like a princess, or at least the way he thought a princess should look. But he did not say so aloud.

The street was crowded with people. Although everyone was muffled against the winter weather, fashionable gentlemen wore their coats cut short in front to expose brocade waistcoats, and knee britches that showed off their calves. Many sported fancy walking-canes which they swung with a careless air. The heavy mantles of the women did not hide the fact that their skirts were draped over large bustles and hooped petticoats.

As they tripped along with mincing steps, their skirts swung like bells and took up a considerable amount of space on the footpath.

Mickser was amused that these grand folk in their ridiculous costumes could not see him. He began making faces at them as they passed; sticking out his tongue, crossing his eyes.

Sophie burst out laughing.

Christmas was in the air, two days hence, and a holiday mood added brilliance to Georgian Dublin.

Instead of the slums Mickser knew, he and Sophie were walking through a growing, thriving city. The Pillar and the General Post Office were missing, but some of the buildings looked oddly familiar to the boy. Now they were shiningly new and clean. By 1907 those still standing would be smoke-blackened and decaying, however, and many would have boarded-up doors. Following the lead of the Duke of Leinster, the affluent area of the city would have long since moved south across the river.

Yet in the wintry light of 1776 Mickser realised for the first time that his Dublin had once been beautiful.

"Sophie?" He gave the toasting fork a tug to get her attention. "What happened to all of this? You've seen where I live. It's Dublin too, but . . . what happened?"

"I cannot say, Mickser. Things change, not always for the better."

"Looks to me like we lost an awful lot."

"Yes," murmured Sophie, thinking of her parents.

Without knowing the reason for it, he sensed her pain. It was his turn to change the subject. "Say, I best be getting back. Mam will be needing me."

"What do you do for her?"

"Lots of things. I pick coal. I search dustbins for bits I can sell, and sometimes I nick food from the shops."

"Nick food . . . you mean, you *steal*?

"If nobody's looking."

Sophie was shocked. "My Papa said we must never, ever take anything that does not belong to us!"

"Hunh. I guess your Papa wasn't never hungry, then," Mickser replied.

CHAPTER NINETEEN

When they returned to the house Garrett was waiting in the hall. "Mademoiselle is looking for you, Miss Sophie," he said in a warning tone as he took her mantle. "With Mr Robert."

She held the toasting fork so he could see it. "I have to put this away first – in the service passage," she added, walking past him before he could ask any more questions.

"That was quick thinking," Mickser told her admiringly.

But as they entered the passage they heard someone hurrying after them. Sophie identified the two sets of footsteps, sharp heels clicking, heavy boots thumping. "My cousin and my governess are right behind us!" Rushing Mickser to the cellar door, she urged him inside, and he lost his hold on the fork.

The world dissolved . . . and reappeared, layer upon layer. Here in the cellar, there was little change, but Sophie had failed to close the door all the way, and as Mickser peered out he could see the two houses – old and new, pristine and filthy, bright and grim – laid one atop the other.

A red-faced man and the sour Mama-zelle caught up with Sophie and began scolding her at once. The boy felt his heart lurch. He knew those voices, those greedy voices. Of course – it was the pair he had heard plotting murder.

And suddenly Mickser knew, with icy certainty, just whose murder they had been plotting.

"You are a very naughty girl," Mademoiselle was saying. "How dare you go out in the cold without telling anyone? You could have made yourself very ill, Sophie. And only two days to your birthday!"

Robert Rutledge added, "We might have had to cancel your party and we cannot allow that, can we? Come, child, there are plans to make. And what is that you have in your hand?"

"Just an old toasting fork. I was about to put it away."

"That again!" cried Mademoiselle in disgust. "You are quite obsessed with the ridiculous thing." Snatching the fork from Sophie's hand, she tossed it into a cupboard and slammed the door.

Robert Rutledge reached past her with a

padlock, which he snapped shut. As both Sophie and Mickser watched aghast, he put the key in his pocket. "That takes care of that," he said. "Now you will go to you, room, and remain there . . ."

"But Cousin Robert . . ."

"Go!" Robert Rutledge snapped. "And I do not wish to hear another word from you."

Mickser stepped through the door as Sophie walked dejectedly down the passage. The boy brushed past Mama-zelle – the woman absently rubbing her arm – and followed the girl. She turned once and looked back, and Mickser smiled and raised his hand in greeting, but the girl turned away, her expression unchanged, and the boy knew then that she couldn't see him.

Sophie turned and went up the stair. Mickser climbed stairs out of both times as he followed her. The effect of the two houses drifting in and out of his vision was sickening and disconcerting. He had to fight to keep down nausea.

He was trapped in the year 1776.

He knew that Sophie's murder had been plotted by those two evil people.

And now he had no way to let her know.

Sophie Rutledge stepped into her bedroom and resisted the temptation to slam the door shut behind her. What had happened to Mickser?

Where was he? And without the fork would he be able to return to his own time? Looking around the room, she said softly, "Mickser?"

She heard a hiss from the window and ran over to pull back the curtains. "Mickser?"

But it was only ice crystals striking against the glass.

"Mickser?"

Something crackled behind her and she whirled, but it was just a coal settling in the grate.

Maybe he had got back safely to this own time. Pulling her shawl tightly around her shoulders, the girl went and sat before the fire on a low stool her father had brought back from the Indies. One of her earliest memories was of sitting on the stool with arms wrapped around her knees, staring into the flames, and seeing figures in the fire. When Mama and Papa were alive, she would often carry the stool into the drawing-room and place it beside her father's chair, so that her back rested against his leg. She would soon nod off, lulled by the gentle murmur of conversation and laughter – there never seemed to be laughter in the house now – and the smell of her father's cigars.

Mickser stood behind Sophie in the room that was – and wasn't – the Mulligan's room. He could see the girl sitting on a low stool before the fire, and beyond her and through her, he could see Mrs Mulligan stirring a pot on the same fire. Behind him, in the elegant bedroom, the twins raced around.

And the boy suddenly realised that not only was he invisible to Sophie, but he was also invisible to the people of his own time.

Kneeling behind the girl, Mickser brought his mouth close to her ear. "Sophie . . ."

The girl brushed at her ear.

"Sophie . . . listen to me Sophie . . ."

The girl moved uncomfortably.

"Oh, Sophie, I've something terrible to tell you . . . but I don't know how . . ." Mickser felt tears of frustration well up in his eyes. He clenched his hands into fists, so hard that his fingernails bit into the hard, callused flesh of his palm. The sudden pain made him cry out . . .

And Sophie looked up, startled.

She had heard something . . . this time she had definitely heard something. Like a cry of pain. Possibly from the street outside, but this was Princess Sophie Mecklenburg Street, rich, safe and elegant, and not the shabby and dangerous Railway Street of Mickser's time.

Drawing her knees up to her chin, the girl stared into the fire, its ruddy glow painting her face blood-red.

. . . danger . . .

. . . terrible danger . . .

The image of a skull appeared in the coals, then melted away, only to reappear in a dozen different places.

. . . you . . .

. . . are . . .

. . . in . . .

. . . terrible . . .

. . . danger . . .

Sophie felt an icy chill walk its way down her spine. For some inexplicable reason she felt frightened . . . no, more than frightened, she was terrified. Though she could not say for what reason.

The image of the skull in the coals remained, mocking her, embers deep in its sockets winking like eyes.

Mickser slumped on the ground, cradling his bloody hands to his chest. The skin was scored and torn where he had dug his nails deeply into his palms, while he screamed and shouted and concentrated furiously on Sophie. She had looked up and looked around, but he doubted if she had heard him.

When he opened his eyes again, he realised that Sophie's house had faded. 19 Railway Street seemed sharper, clearer now, like an image viewed through gauze.

The boy scrambled to his feet and staggered from the room. This time he actually felt the presence of the door as he stepped through. It was like walking through glue. Maybe he didn't need that old toasting fork to bring him back to his own time, he told himself with growing excitement.

Mickser flowed down the two flights of stairs, passing right through a white-capped maid carrying a tray upstairs. The girl jumped as if she had been bitten by a flea.

At the bottom of the stairs, the boy turned to the left. As he approached the cellar, Granny Hayes's door opened and the old woman stepped out. She stopped, blind eye turning towards him . . . then she frowned and shook her head, and continued down the passage toward the backyard.

Mickser descended the cellar steps, trying desperately hard not to think about what he was going to do.

At the bottom of the stairs, he stood with his back to the wall, breathing deeply. Now that the pain from his torn hands was fading, he noticed that Sophie's house seemed to be coming back into clearer focus.

Suddenly, he brought both elbows back and rammed them as hard as he could against the stone wall.

The pain was excruciating.

CHAPTER TWENTY

"Mickser, where were you . . . I've been looking everywhere for you." Thomas Lawless met his brother on the stairs. The younger boy's face was sickly, contrasting sharply with his red-rimmed eyes.

"What's wrong?" Mickser asked through clenched teeth. "Has someone been fighting with you again? If they have I'll kill them," he said. Though not at the moment, he added silently; both arms felt numb from the elbows down.

"It's Daddy," whispered Thomas, eyes suddenly huge behind welling tears. In that instant Mickser forgot all his pain. Brushing past his younger brother, he pounded up the stairs and burst into their room – the guest bedroom, he recalled bitterly.

The room was crowded with people and he knew instantly that it was bad – very bad. Most were neighbours from the other rooms, some were relatives of his mother's; there were none of his father's people alive anymore. All their heads were bent, and thick black rosary beads clicked softly. Nan Lawless was standing at the foot of the bed, supported between Mad Alice and Granny Hayes. The three women were stony-faced as they watched the black-coated priest bend over the man in the bed.

The boy stopped.

He was going to throw up, he could feel his stomach churning . . . while he had been gallivanting around some dream Dublin, his father had died, and he hadn't been there!

He hadn't been *here*.

And he should have been.

His place was here.

The boy squeezed his hands into fists, re-opening the fresh wounds. Blood trickled from between his fingers and dripped onto the floor; but the pain cleared his head.

Mickser saw his mother looking at him and made his way through the crowd towards her. She opened her arms and gathered him to her. He blinked furiously, determined not to cry, but he could feel his tears soaking into the thin cotton of her blouse. "Mam?" he whispered. "Mam?"

Nan Lawless pressed her face against her son's head and held him tightly. One of her tears trickled down his forehead, then down his cheek. When it touched his lips he licked them automatically. The taste was salty and bitter.

"Your Daddy took bad this morning," she said. "The priest has come to give him the last rites. I don't think he'll last through the day." Nan raised her head and looked at her husband, lying unmoving in the centre of the bed. The only indication that he was still alive was the gentle rise and fall of his chest. "I had wanted him to see one more Christmas," she said wistfully, her breath warm against Mickser's head. "Just one more Christmas as a family. One more Christmas."

CHAPTER TWENTY-ONE

Sophie awoke with a tingle of anticipation. "Today I am sixteen years old!" she exclaimed as she sat up in bed and stretched.

The chambermaid responded with a half-hearted smile. It had been a long time since she was sixteen years old, and her future had never been as bright as Sophie's. "Yes, Miss, today is Christmas Eve. It is very cold outside, but your fire is lit and your pitcher is filled with warm water. Is there anything else?"

"Where is Mademoiselle?"

The maid rubbed her sooty hands on the towel tucked in the waistband of her apron. "In the library, I believe, with Mr Robert. Shall I fetch her for you?"

"No! That is . . . no. I apologise for snapping at you, Elizabeth. I only meant I do not care to see Mademoiselle."

"We none of us do, Miss," the maid assured her. She curtsied quickly as she left the room.

Washed and dressed, Sophie made her way down to the dining-room. She paused in front of the big mirror in the hall. She was just patting a curl into place when she recalled Mickser's face peering over her shoulder in the same glass. Her good mood evaporated. "How will I ever find you again without the toasting fork?" she whispered across the centuries.

For one brief moment clouds swirled in the glass. Then they were gone. Sophie rubbed her hand across her eyes and looked again but the mirror was perfectly clear.

Oh, Mickser, where are you now? *When* are you?

Today his Daddy would die.

Mickser sat on the bottom step of the cellar, head bent between his knees, hands locked over the back of his head.

"Today my Daddy will die."

He simply had to get away from the room. There had been a constant stream of people coming and going over the past day. Some he knew; most were strangers. But everyone brought a little gift, a loaf of bread, a few scraps of meat, a stone jar of porter, a little bottle of snuff. It had taken him a while before he realised that they were bringing supplies for the wake. His father was still alive and breathing, but they were thinking of him as if he was already dead. That had made him angry. And then his anger turned to rage when he saw his mother carefully piling up the gifts instead of using the food and drink right now, when they were most needed.

Feeling lost and heartbroken, Mickser had wandered through the house. He wished he could forget what was happening. But everywhere he went people were talking about his dying father, asking him how he was, how his mother was, how baby Emma and little Thomas were.

No one asked how he was.

It was snowing outside – it was going to be a white Christmas – but Mickser hated snow. It covered everything, so you couldn't see the stones on the road or the chips in the cobbles, and the icy cold burned your feet. Unable to go out, he had finally wandered down to the cellar where it was still and silent and peaceful.

Sitting in the gloom, he suddenly thought of Sophie.

And felt guilty.

He hadn't warned her. Hadn't managed to let her know that her cousin and Mama-zelle were plotting her murder . . . this very night!

The boy got to his feet with a look of grim

resolution. She was still alive then. There was something he could do, even if he couldn't save his father.

Hurrying down the last step, ignoring the squeaking rats, Mickser delved into the rubbish where he had hidden the toasting fork that existed in his own time.

The day passed in a whirl of excitement. Sophie was busy every minute, preoccupied with the party to come.

After lunch Mademoiselle presented Sophie with a little package wrapped in silver tissue. "A tiny remembrance for your birthday, open it when you open the others," she said with a smile. "Perhaps you will forgive me our misunderstandings, *oui*? I should like us to be friends from now on, Sophie."

"Of course, *Mademoiselle*," Sophie smiled.

In mid-afternoon the governess sent Sophie upstairs to change into her party clothes. "I suggest one of those new imported Indian cottons from the dressmaker. They are more becoming than anything else you have."

"Is December not the wrong season for cotton, Mademoiselle?"

"*Non non*, I assure you the fabric is very fashionable now in Paris. Besides, you will be quite hot from excitement. Do wear a cotton frock, Sophie – perhaps the pale blue one? And the pearls of your dear *Maman*, of course."

The first guests to arrive were Clara and Louise Maunsel, Sophie's oldest friends, together with their elder brother James. Within moments the three girls were holding hands and giggling together. Sophie took her guests into the drawing-room, where a large crystal bowl waited with hot punch. Garrett ladled out a drink for each of the young people with as much formality as he would have shown at any adult party.

Sophie felt very grand. She began to wish she had worn the pearls as Mademoiselle suggested. Seeing the Maunsel girls in velvet, she felt underdressed in her Indian cotton. She had chosen the cameo that her father had given her on her last birthday before he . . . before he died. She deliberately didn't pursue that thought and concentrated on her reflection in the mirror. She decided that the cameo brooch looked much better than pearls with her low-necked cotton frock.

Then Louise Maunsel gave a little shriek and dropped her cup. Crimson punch splashed over the Turkish carpet. "Somebody touched me!" she exclaimed, putting one hand to the back of her neck. "I felt an icy finger, just here!"

"Half a cupful of punch and you're drunk," James, her brother, teased.

Only Sophie didn't join in the laughter.

Sophie.

Sophie.

Mickser wasn't entirely sure what had happened. He'd been holding the toasting fork, turning it over and over in his hands, thinking furiously about Sophie and 19 Princess Sophie Mecklenburg Street, wishing he was there, desperately wishing he could help her. One of the metal tines on the fork had caught in the torn flesh of his palm . . .

And suddenly the world had shifted.

And another layer had appeared.

And the cellar had a door again.

There was a party going on in the house. The boy could hear voices raised high in laughter. Mickser wandered into the front room. Three overdressed girls and a boy dressed to look like an old man stood laughing and giggling together before the blazing fire.

And superimposed over them, Mickser could see fragments of the family of eight who now occupied the room.

It took him a moment to recognise Sophie. With her copper hair piled atop her head, wearing a low-cut gown that exposed much of her shoulders, she looked very much the young woman. In that instant the boy realised that she was probably the most beautiful person he had ever seen. Oh, there were plenty of pretty women who walked Railway Street and around Monto, but their beauty came from bottles and cheap perfume. Sophie Rutledge was simply beautiful.

And tonight she would die.

As the boy attempted to get close to her, he brushed past one of the giggling girls, who squealed and dropped her cup.

In addition to friends of her own age, Sophie had invited Colonel and Mrs Maunsel and some of the other neighbours. The Maunsels arrived almost an hour after their children, brushing snow from their clothes as they entered. By that time the party was at its height. On a table in the drawing-room a pile of beribboned birthday presents waited. Laughing, chattering young people wandered through the house, drinking punch and mulled wine and dropping bits of Christmas cake onto the rugs, while the adults listened to hired musicians play chamber music.

19 Mecklenburg Street was alive with light and gaiety.

And no one but Mickser saw the grim ghosts of its future. The boy shadowed Sophie, sticking as close to her as he could. He had tried and tried and tried to get her attention, but failed. On a couple of occasions he had come close and she had turned suddenly, eyes wide, searching, but was unable to see him. A couple of the other guests had felt his presence though, he was sure of that; they had shivered as he went past, scratching at suddenly goose-pimpled skin, sipping suddenly sour wine.

Cousin Robert paid Sophie extravagant compliments. "You bloom like a Christmas rose, you quite take my breath away. I am very devoted to you, my angel," he gushed, putting an arm around her shoulders for all to see. When she unwrapped her presents his was the most impressive of all: a small mahogany curio cabinet already supplied with a collection of exotic seashells.

But when she saw the shells, Sophie's eyes brimmed with tears. They were a too-painful reminder of the sea which had swallowed her parents.

Only Mrs Maunsel, who had been her mother's dearest friend, understood. "You must not weep, Sophie," she said gently. "Your parents would want you to be happy this evening."

Sophie forced a smile. "I am happy," she insisted. Turning away she took another present from the table. Mademoiselle's. But when she opened the package, it contained only an inexpensive hair ribbon.

Robert Rutledge rang the service bell to attract attention. Gathering the crowd in the drawing-room, he announced, "It is time to begin the party games. Shall we start with hide-and-seek?"

Mickser attempted to get close to Sophie, but the large number of people were crowding in on him, around him, confusing him, and in the drawing-room of 19 Railway Street, the huge Carroll clan were gathering to celebrate Christmas.

"Since it is your birthday, Sophie, you must hide first," Robert continued.

Sophie eagerly agreed. As her guests covered their eyes, she turned and ran from the room.

It took Mickser a few moments before he realised that she was gone.

And by the time he made his way into the hall, Sophie had vanished.

As Sophie crossed the hall Mademoiselle stepped out of the cloakroom. She had a shawl draped around her shoulders. "I know the perfect hiding place for you," the Frenchwoman whispered, linking an arm through hers.

"I was going upstairs to hide in the big wardrobe in the rose bedroom."

"That is too easy, they would find you at once. *Non non*, come with me, I insist." She gave Sophie a warm, encouraging smile. "I am very good at games, as you will see. I know the perfect hiding place. Where no one will ever find you."

CHAPTER TWENTY-TWO

Keeping up a steady stream of friendly conversation, Mademoiselle led the way to the back stairs. This time her destination was not the cellar. With a lamp in one hand and the girl following her she ascended to the very top of the house. At last she halted, panting a little, on the uppermost landing, and set down her lamp.

Two doors faced onto this landing, one on either side.

Sophie was puzzled. "You think I should hide in the attic? But surely . . ."

"Not the attic, *chérie*. I have an even better place in mind, one that will offer your friends a challenge." Reaching into her pocket, the governess produced a key and brandished it in the lamplight. "This opens the door onto the roof." She inserted the key in the right-hand door and turned the lock.

"You cannot be serious. It is cold out there,

Mademoiselle!" Sophie shrank back, but the governess caught her by the wrist.

"Nonsense, look at you, your face is quite flushed. A little fresh air will do you good. Take my shawl to wrap around you and stand in the angle, out of the wind. You will be quite comfortable until someone finds you." Ignoring Sophie's protests, she pushed her through the door and out onto a flat area of the roof.

The girl stepped into a twilit world of swirling snow. A gust of cold wind hit her full in the face, making her cough. She put one hand over her mouth as a lady should, and turned to go back in spite of the governess . . .

. . . just as the door slammed in her face.

For one brief moment Sophie thought it was an accident and that the wind had slammed the door.

Then she heard the key turning in the lock.

Frantically, she began pounding on the door with her fists. "Mademoiselle, I do not want to do this! Let me back in!"

There was no answer. Only the sound of footsteps retreating down the stairs.

When Robert saw the governess slip back into the drawing-room, he excused himself and headed for the library, still carrying his mulled port. He was glad to find the room empty of guests for the moment. Soon Annette Moulin joined him there, closing the doors behind her.

"Is it done?" he asked in a low voice.

"The girl is locked on the roof. With the noise of the party in here, and the wind howling outside, even if she screams no one will hear her."

He took out his pocket watch and noted the time. "I shall go up in an hour and, ahem, find her. Poor Sophie, frozen stiff. What a terrible accident."

Mademoiselle shook her head. "A healthy girl will not freeze to death as quickly as all that. But she will be weakened by then; you can smother her with my shawl."

The colour drained from his face and he sipped the port quickly. "I cannot kill her with my bare hands, Annette!"

"Can you not?" Annette Moulin's smile was bitter, cynical. "Think of all that lovely money, Robert! All that stands between us and a fortune is one stupid little girl." Her long-fingered hands moved as she described a tightening knot. "Close your eyes and think of the money," she whispered. "Think of owning this house and everything in it . . . and all your gambling debts cleared. And think of me. Think of me, Robert. And all that stands between us and fortune is up there . . ." She silently raised her face to the ceiling.

Robert Rutledge brought the glass to his lips

and drained the remainder of the port – then abruptly turned and spat the liquid into the fire, where it briefly blazed and roared. "Gone sour," he said, wiping his chin. Mademoiselle turned away to hide her disgust.

Mickser had been just about to return to the cellar and his own time when he saw Robert leaving the drawing-room. The boy had almost convinced himself that there would be no attempt on Sophie's life – there couldn't be, not with so many people about.

Anyway, he needed to get back to his own time.

He had to be there when his father . . . when his father . . .

The boy shook his head savagely. He wasn't going to think about that.

But when he discovered that Mama-zelle had locked Sophie on the roof, he knew that they did intend to kill her. He recalled the flimsy dress she'd been wearing. She was going to freeze to death.

Pushing his way through the door, the boy desperately began to make his way to the top of the house.

Meanwhile Sophie's friends were seeking their hostess. They looked in all the obvious places –

including the wardrobes – but could not find her. The Gardiner girls grew tired of the game and began playing whist in the drawing-room. Some of the young people joined them, while others continued the search.

At last James Maunsel suggested, "What if Sophie has gone up to the attic?"

Mademoiselle hastily said, "Only servants go into that part of the house. Sophie would never go there, particularly not in a party frock."

"Our Sophie is very clever," Robert Rutledge added. "I promise you she has hidden herself away under your very noses, and will let you search until the very last one gives up. Then she will pop out and make you feel foolish!"

Spurred by his words, they redoubled their efforts. But no one even came close to finding the girl.

The higher he got the more difficult it became. Climbing the stairs had been a nightmare; he'd been unsure if he was stepping on steps in his own time or in Sophie's. Once he'd put his foot right through a solid step . . . until he remembered that in his own time there was a gaping hole just there. Looking down, he discovered that his leg was pin-cushioned with splinters. But he'd no time to remove them. He had to get to Sophie.

Before it was too late.

CHAPTER TWENTY-THREE

No matter how tightly she hugged herself Sophie could not get warm. She shouted and then screamed, she beat the door with her fists until they were bruised and bloody, but no one heard. No one came.

She was alone with the night and the raging snowstorm.

For a time she tried to comfort herself with the knowledge that her friends were searching for her. Soon they would think of looking in the attic. Soon they would come up the stairs.

But her voice was growing hoarse. Would they be able to hear her through the heavy door?

The snow was falling more thickly than ever as she struggled to understand what had happened. Was it possible Mademoiselle was trying to kill her? But why?

And if not, why had she been locked out to freeze to death?

Sophie fought against a rising tide of panic. Her heart was hammering so hard she could scarcely breathe. Wrapping the flimsy shawl around her head, and gathering all her courage, the girl inched to the edge of the roof and looked down. Below was darkness and hard pavement. A misstep and she would fall to her death.

Turning, she went back to the locked door and leaned her forehead against it in despair. The pain in her hands and feet was growing intense now, a burning sensation like fire. She couldn't feel her cheeks and when she blinked her eyes it hurt. "Mama," she whispered. "Oh, Papa."

"Sophie."

The girl jumped. But it wasn't her father's voice she had heard.

"Mickser!"

For a moment the solid door shimmered, turned rotten and warped, and then a hand briefly appeared. In an eyeblink it vanished again.

"I'm here," said Mickser Lawless.

Crouching in the angle of the chimneys, Sophie was shivering so badly she could barely talk. She couldn't see Mickser in front of her, though she could hear his sonorous breathing. "I am going to die here, Mickser."

The boy said nothing.

"Maybe I shall die here and in your own time you can come up to this place, here, in the angle of the chimneys and find my bones."

"Don't say that."

"Because of course in your time, I'm already dead."

The wind changed direction, whirling snow around the girl. Her thin cotton dress was almost soaked through and clinging wetly to her skin, which was now tinged with blue.

"I tried to warn people," Mickser said desperately, "but they can't hear me. Some of them seem to be able to feel me or my presence . . ."

"So that was you downstairs!" she exclaimed. "But how did you get back here to my time?"

"I wished myself back. I had the fork, but you weren't there to hold it. I wanted to try and help you. Not that I've done much good," he added bitterly.

"And your father, Mickser," Sophie asked through chattering teeth, "how is your father?"

"He's going to die tonight," the boy said flatly.

"You should go to him," Sophie replied.

"My mother is there. He won't die alone. I won't leave you here . . ." He left the sentence unfinished, but Sophie finished it for him.

"You will not leave me here to die alone."

143

"Oh Sophie, I wish there was something I could do!"

"So do I, Mickser, so do I. I'm so cold . . . so cold."

The girl heard shuffling in the snow, then something – not a snowflake – brushed her cheek. It felt almost like a hand.

Closing his eyes, breathing deeply, then holding his breath, Mickser squeezed his hand into a fist – and then pounded the fist into the roof. The pain was excruciating. White-hot fire burned up his wrist and into his elbow and shoulder, but Mickser welcomed the pain.

Pain had brought him back to this time, and that same pain now anchored him to this world.

He was here.

Really here.

While the pain lasted.

Suddenly he could feel the snow on his face, could feel his breath pluming coldly on the air.

"Mickser," Sophie breathed, as the apparition began to flicker into sight directly before her. "How did you do that?"

"You do not want to know," the boy said through gritted teeth. Then, gathering the girl into his arms, he held her close, willing the heat from his body, from his Railway Street, into her chill flesh.

Sophie wrapped her arms around the boy. Gratefully she felt precious, unbelievable heat soak into her body. "You should go home, Mickser, you should go back to your father."

"I can't do anything for him. But maybe I can do something for you. Even if I can only hold you."

"That's enough," she whispered, "that's more than enough."

CHAPTER TWENTY-FOUR

In the midst of the party, establishing his alibi, Robert Rutledge waited with barely concealed impatience for the hour to pass. When Sophie had still not appeared, he waited another half hour for good measure.

By that time Mrs Maunsel was becoming anxious. "Surely they should have found her by now, Robert. Should you not ask one of the servants to look for her? Perhaps she has fallen asleep somewhere."

"What girl would fall asleep at her own birthday party? No, I tell you, she is simply hiding very successfully and having a good laugh on us all. But if you are so concerned, I shall go look for her myself. In just a few minutes."

He drank another tumbler of mulled wine and ate another slice of Cook's fruitcake. Then at last he made a great show of setting off in search of Sophie. Starting at the bottom of the house.

Old Colonel Maunsel disapproved. "When I was a lad," he told anyone who would listen, "I always went up. Always. Up trees, up poles, up stairs. I tell you, that girl is hiding above us somewhere, in the maids' rooms under the eaves perhaps."

Robert Rutledge disagreed. Only with the greatest reluctance did he finally enlarge the search to include the upper stories of the house. And then he spent the longest possible time in every room before going on to the next one – or letting anyone else go either. When he could put it off no longer, he said he would look in the attic.

To his dismay, Garrett announced, "I shall come with you, Sir."

Mademoiselle stepped forward. "Oh, but you must not! Miss Sophie would be so embarrassed, having one of the servants come after her as if she were still a child."

Robert threw her a grateful glance. "Garrett," he ordered, "you stay here and look after our guests. If Sophie is up there I shall escort her down myself, I need no help."

He hurried off toward the service passage, but once out of sight of the others he moved much more slowly. He took up a lamp and began to climb the back stairs. As he climbed, he gnawed on his lower lip like a man facing a task he dreads.

When Robert reached the roof door he saw that his accomplice had left the key in the lock. He put one ear to the wood and listened, but heard nothing. Even the wind had died down. He squared his shoulders, turned the key, and eased the door open.

At first he saw only darkness and the reflection of the lamplight on the swirling snowflakes. He shuddered as the chill wind bit through his clothing. Then he made out a huddled figure in the snow. "Sophie?"

As he started toward her, she moaned.

Robert raised the lamp high over his head so he could see her face. "Sophie?" he asked again. Flickering yellow light bathed the girl . . . then her eyes snapped open and she was looking straight at him. He had been hoping to find her dead, but she was very much alive.

She must realise that Mademoiselle had locked her out on purpose. She had to die now, before she could tell anyone.

But how? She had the shawl wrapped tightly around her body and he was reluctant to pull it free. He really did not want to touch her. Touching her would make it terribly real.

"Why did you not simply die the way I wanted?" he asked miserably.

Sophie's voice was hoarse and exhausted, yet when she spoke he could hear every word she said. Her words beat at him, condemning him. "Why do you want me to die, Cousin Robert?"

"Because you are in my way!" he cried at the girl. "The entire Rutledge estate is yours now and it should be mine. What does a stupid girl know of money? You would waste it on fripperies and hair ribbons. But that fortune will set me free."

"The entire estate? I did not know. I will give you whatever you want, you do not have to kill me."

"But I do. I have to now . . . I have no choice. Annette says . . ." He advanced toward her again.

Sophie threw up her hands to ward him off. "Please, no!"

She looked so small crouching there; so helpless. She was one of his own, with the red Rutledge hair and the square Rutledge chin. In other circumstances he might have been genuinely fond of her. But she was such a child compared to Annette, who knew so many ways to charm a man.

He could not afford sentiment, he was too deeply in debt. Besides, he had promised to give the governess a share of the fortune for helping him. Annette Moulin would never let him back down. He knew the woman; if he spared Sophie now she would gladly send him to prison for revenge.

He would have to go through with the murder.

As he reached for Sophie she scrambled to her feet. She was not as weak as he thought. It would not be possible to smother her with the shawl, she would struggle too hard.

But if he moved quickly, he could throw her off the roof. It would be a terrible, tragic accident.

CHAPTER TWENTY-FIVE

Robert Routledge, Sophie's cousin appeared.

Mickser knew the type. A bully, a coward . . . and now, about to be a murderer.

Mickser threw back his head and shouted aloud, but the wind and time whipped away his words. He screamed and shouted . . . then he pounded his injured hand into the rooftop again.

Sophie was on her feet, backing away from her cousin. Robert saw her terrified gaze turn toward the door and he smiled insolently. He stepped to one side, blocking her escape. It must look as if she were accidentally locked out up here and wandered too close to the edge of the roof in the snowstorm. He glanced down to see how near they were to the edge. The falling snow would cover any footprints.

That was when he saw the footprints.

Footprints coming towards him across

undisturbed snow. First one and then another, as if someone was advancing on him.

And beside each bare-toed footprint, a speckling of bright red blood.

But there was no one there!

No one.

Robert shook his head. A trick of the light, no doubt. His hand trembling violently, he held the lamp forwards for a better look.

The footprints continued to come straight towards him.

Snow whirled and shifted and for an instant seemed to stick to something. When the snow flurried again, it started to paint itself onto a ghostly shape, black and almost invisible, one half faintly etched in snow.

A hand materialised in front of Robert. A bloody hand, the knuckles torn, blood seeping from beneath ragged fingernails. Blood dripped from the hand to stain the snow.

With a strangled cry, the man took a step back. His eyes bulged with terror as he sought frantically to see something which was not there. Which should not be there. With absolute certainty he knew there were now three beings on the roof.

"Sophie," he whispered, "do you see it?"

"Yes, I see it."

"What is it?"

"My friend."

Robert took another step backward as the near invisible, bloody-handed horror drew closer. Step after step. On it came. Gibbering in fright, Robert Rutledge retreated. The low parapet at the edge of the roof touched the back of his calves but he did not notice. He was only aware of his unseen pursuer, this red-handed doom bearing down on him.

The footprints stopped right in front of him.

There was only the lamp between them, and the light which revealed nothing.

A breeze colder than the December wind blew across his face. Robert Rutledge leaned backward, trying to avoid its icy breath. Back and back until . . . his arms windmilled wildly but it was too late. In absolute terror, the man felt the world tilt beneath him and he began to fall.

Just as he went over the edge he finally saw, for one heart-stopping moment, the figure of a boy fully outlined in falling snow.

CHAPTER TWENTY-SIX

Mickser was cold. Colder than he had ever been in his life. And dripping wet.

Mickser came to his feet with a yelp, then swore as his injured hand banged against the wall. He was standing in a pool of melted snow. Individual snowflakes still clung to his hair and cheeks like crystal tears.

He was back in the cellar, in his own time, and Sophie . . .

Even as he was thinking of her, she appeared, but faintly, very faintly, shimmering like a candle flame before him. And she was older now. Much older, with snowy hair and a tiny pair of spectacles on her nose.

"I knew I would find you here, Mickser. It is Christmas Eve again in both our worlds. But in your world it is still 1907, in mine it is 1825."

"I don't understand . . ."

"I know now that you used your pain to bring you back to my time; it took me a long time to realise that love would do the same. I have loved you dearly all my life . . . it is the same love which allows me to speak to you now. You saved my life, Mickser. Cousin Robert broke his neck that night when he fell off the roof. It was the fate he meant for me."

"What happened then? I don't remember; it's all . . . blurry."

"Cousin Robert screamed as he fell. Garrett heard him and ran outside to find the body. Then he came up to the roof with Norman and Colonel Maunsel and found me. I was ill for a while afterward, but when I got better I told everyone what had happened. Except the part about you, of course. I did not think anyone would believe that."

"The Frenchwoman, what about her?"

"When Mademoiselle realised my cousin was dead, she took advantage of the confusion to run away that same night. None of us ever saw her again, though I later read a story about a Frenchwoman convicted of enticing a man to murder. It might have been the same person." The woman was growing even more dim. Mickser could hardly see her at all.

"Wait!" he cried, holding out his hands imploringly. "Don't go!"

"Ah, Mickser, I have been gone a long time. But I left something behind. Listen to me."

He strained to hear her words. They seemed to be coming from very far away.

"That Christmas Eve I became a wealthy woman. I put some money aside to repay you for my life." Her voice faded to a whisper. "Gold sovereigns . . . in a bag . . . "

She was gone! He could not see her at all!

Then her voice came to him one final time across the centuries, as sweet and clear as if she stood beside him. "At the angle of the chimneys, Mickser. At the angle of the chimneys."

CHAPTER TWENTY-SEVEN

It was snowing again.

One hundred and thirty years later and it was snowing.

For a moment, Mickser imagined that he was back on the roof again, with the snow whirling down, holding the shivering Sophie, and whispering his secrets to her, telling her all the things he wanted to do, all the places he wanted to see, and finally admitting to her that he never would.

How long ago had he held her – 130 years – or ten minutes? He could still feel the weight of her against him, smell the fresh sweetness of her hair, feel the gentle thumping of her heartbeat against his.

As he walked across the snow, his footsteps mimicking the steps he had taken so long ago, he half expected Cousin Robert to appear and pitch him off the roof. But Cousin Robert and his world were long gone. Sophie's world too was long gone, and he and his family and the others like them were living in their shadow.

This was the place where he had held Sophie, this corner here, this angle of chimneys. She had joked that he might find her bones here. He was terrified to realise just how close that had come to being the truth.

Mickser scraped away the piled snow and then dug deeply into generations of bird droppings, searching for he knew not what. Who was to say that it was still here, after all those years . . .

His questing fingers touched leather.

Could be a dead bird, a mummified rat, he reasoned, trying not to get his hopes up too far. He pulled it out.

It was a bag. A bulging leather bag tied tightly with cord.

His numb fingers fumbled with the cord, but it was stuck fast and he finally wrenched it free with his teeth. Reaching in, he touched cold metal, thick paper and a brooch of some kind.

The boy lifted out the brooch first and smiled in remembrance. This was the cameo Sophie had been wearing that night. He remembered the pressure of it against his chest. Tilting the bag to the light, he looked in . . . and saw the gold sovereigns and a folded letter.

He saw food . . .

. . . and medicine. . . .

He saw his father living.

19, Princess Sophie Mecklenburg Street,
Dublin

Dear Mickser,

If I am right, you will be reading this in Nineteen Railway Street. I hope you will remember the house as it was, and as it could be again.

Nothing need ever be lost, Mickser, not if we are willing to fight for it. You fought for my life. Now I want you to use this money to fight for your father's life. There is more than enough here to buy medicine and food. Do not let anyone throw you and your family out into the street. This is your home, as it was mine.

After that fateful Christmas Eve I went abroad for a while. When I returned to Dublin I was very lonely. I missed you. But you were far away. Eventually I married James Maunsel in this very house; you might remember him, he was at that party. Our children were born here. They have since scattered to the four corners of the earth: two to Bristol, one to Belgium, one all the way to the new nation of America. Our eldest son is a solicitor in London. His address is on the sealed envelope enclosed with this letter. I pray the firm he founded will still be a thriving concern in 1907.

My dear husband passed away many years ago. I live on at Nineteen Mecklenburg Street, alone except for my devoted servants. I am a very old lady now. But I often think of my youth. Not a day has gone by when I did not think of you.

In this bag you will find not only some money, but my favourite cameo. Send the cameo, together with the sealed letter, to the solicitors in London. The cameo will identify you to them, and the letter will explain what I wish to be done. I have left a larger legacy which they are to pay out to you gradually, in ways that will cause no suspicion.

Mickser, I want you to go back to school and get an education. When you are a man, I want you to travel, I want you to see all those places we talked about that night, those places that you thought you might never see. And when you are done with your travels, buy this old house and restore it to something of its former grandeur. Live in it and be happy here as I have been. And, sometimes,

Remember me.
Ever your loving friend,
Sophie

Also published by Poolbeg

Vampyre

by

Michael Scott

It begins with the gift of an ancient bone comb Robert gives his girlfriend, Karen. In the days that follow, Karen's dreams are vivid and strange. She is haunted by images of a red-haired girl who terrifyingly seems to be aware of Karen. Her dreams become darker and wilder until there are times when she finds it hard to distinguish reality from fantasy. Is she dreaming of the red-haired girl . . . or is she seeing into the past?

Robert becomes aware of the changes in Karen. He begins noticing subtle changes in her. But it is only when he discovers the puncture marks in the crook of his arm that he realises what Karen has become – a vampyre!

The vampyre hasn't yet totally possessed Karen and in a desperate race against time, Robert attempts to banish the creature, but he is pitted against one of the oldest enemies of mankind . . .

ISBN: 1 85371 545 X

Also published by Poolbeg

Cold Places

by

Morgan Llywelyn

When David McHugh discovers an unexpected talent for finding what he calls "cold places" – sites that have ancient power – it isn't long until he locates a valuable artefact buried in one of these sites. The find excites his father, a professor of archaeology. David is pleased to have made his father proud of him, but soon becomes frightened. As his "pull" to cold places becomes stronger, David discovers that these freezing energy vortexes provide a direct link to the Ice Age and he finds himself uncontrollably slipping into the past, terrified of being unable to return to the present. Worse yet, the malevolent ice follows him back to his own time!

With his girlfriend, Molly Doyle, he tries to find a way to stop the influence the spirit of the ice is having on modern weather. But while he is battling strange forces, he is also struggling to grow up and accept the changes that are taking place in his own life.

ISBN: 1 85371 541 7